The Bedford Compe

Anthology 2020

Featuring stories by:

Norma Allen, Chris Barkley, Robert Carter, Paul Chiswick, Anya Christiansen, Sarah Dawson, Amanda Hildebrandt, Juliet Hill, Sophie Holland, Fran Maciver, Shirley Smith Matheson, Janet Newman, Pauline Plummer, David Shelley Jones, Kirsten Udall, James Woolf

and

poems by:

Maya Abraham-Steele, Alba Alonso Palombi, Wura Arisekola, Maia Béar, Anne Casey, Tamsin Hopkins, Joseph Kidney, Vanessa Lampert, Isabella Mead, Federica Peru, Harriet Sanders, Han Smith, Molly Underwood, Ben Verinder

ISBN: 978-1-8382586-2-7

Published in paperback by

OSTRICH BOOKS

www.ostrichbooks.co.uk

First published in Great Britain 2021

Printed by IngramSpark
Cover photograph courtesy of Helen Hall

Foreword by the Chair of The Bedford Competition

Frank McMahon

My very sincere thanks to all who made this anthology possible: our competition judges for their time, wisdom and inspirational advice. Their attention to detail and determination to reveal the worthy and eventual winners from a compilation of impressive candidates was commendable and much appreciated.

Thanks also to our readers for their time and dedication in helping compile a long list of short stories for our judges to consider. It really was a challenge, but they were not found wanting and deserve the highest praise for their commitment and perseverance.

With entries from over thirty countries exceeding expectations, we have been able to make a significant donation to Age UK Bedfordshire for their covid-19 emergency appeal.

It has been a privilege and a pleasure to read and reflect on the myriad scenarios which these writers presented. I hope you will marvel at and enjoy the fruits of their creative imaginations as much as we have.

Finally, my particular thanks to my colleagues Maureen Hanrahan, Marie Coles and Philip Carey for all their hard work, and to all our many local supporters who have enabled us to complete a very successful competition.

Contents

2020 SHORT STORY COMPETITION

Short Story Competition Judge's Report

Jordan Lees

I had a lot of fun judging the short story competition this year. I'd definitely like to thank Bedford Competition and all the authors who entered; it was a really interesting and very welcome distraction from the world. The standard was extremely high and it took me a long time to whittle the shortlist down. There was a great range of subject matter and writing styles. And it just made it really tough. As an agent, I do a lot of reading every day of the week, but I can genuinely say it was so much fun reading the stories, as well as being a challenge.

My choice for third place was *The life and Times of Sam the Wanderer as the end of Days Approaches*. It is a really poignant story, but there's also this real tension in it straight away because we are, as readers, really grasping at what kind of catastrophe has occurred for all manner of basic things to have disappeared and add into that the spectre of the dogs. It is a real masterclass in trauma within such a short framework. It uses characters to really and subtly unpack the gravity of that change. The language is very contained, but beautiful throughout.

In second place, I chose *Beacons*. I loved this as a wonderful dynamic play throughout between this real sense of humour, and profound sadness. It is perfectly balanced between both. The core is the idea of language, vanishing and becoming obsolete. But that is used as a vehicle to explore a much more terrifying and troubling concept, which is that the beauty of the natural world itself is escaping our consciousness. It is done through the lens of a father trying to reconnect with his daughter, trying to understand each other. It moved me and made me laugh. It was outstanding.

The first place, *Mångata* is an outstanding piece of writing. It does so many things at once. It is mysterious, tense, very thoughtful and just so elegant. I love the concept of having to leave something behind if you take something. It is just very charged with meaning within the context of the story but also charged within a broader, bigger way about our place in the world and our lives. There is so much depth and breadth in a few pages. It has got lots of flair, but it is also very precise. It was a pleasure to still be thinking about it long after I had finished reading it.

WINNER

Mångata

Chris Barkley

Euan walks down to Camasunary Bay. His pack sways like a lazy metronome, he treads in time. The path is etched with land veins that weave from a high loch down to the sea. Day sets down its instruments and there is a pause, a tuning, before the night begins its movement. Euan strides through the interval, through the unfurling dusk wind, towards the bay. The sea ebbs in his skin like a blood-bruise. Not far now.

He looks down at the bay, bordered by mountains that circle like wary dogs, spines arched and pale. There is a structure; an ink smear on the land that wavers in the salt-mist. He knows it from his childhood. Bothy-hopping, his father called it; wandering across the country, sleeping in these abandoned places at the edge of the world. Growing up, he and his family had stayed in so many. Now, he is returning to them, one by one. This is the last.

The land flattens as the dark moon opens like a seal's eye. The bothy coils from the ink smear, a quiet sentinel looking out to sea. The ground is boggy, and Euan feels the grey mud seep through his boots and wet his socks as he treads on. Ahead, the door comes into view. A memory: he and his sister racing to be the first inside. Natasha. He sees her now, bolting ahead, silhouette shrinking. She bursts inside and closes the door behind her. She is singing a song to tease him. He hears her now, as he rests his grimed hand on the doorlatch. He throws open the door.

No one there. Two empty rooms yawn at him, one with a table, another with a raised platform for sleeping. He slings off his pack and lays it on the table, taking out his stove. He boils some pasta, and in the amber stove light, watches through the window as the waves blur the shoreline. There is a thrust of shattered stone that wends out into the sea; a finger of land seeking another.

He rubs his eyes, tired from the long walk. Standing, he gazes around the bothy and sees a glimmer in the corner. A metal box. Paint flakes from it, and in the dark wells, rust bristles like mould. There is no lock. Anyone may stay in a bothy; there is no knowing who could have left it. Wreathed in the flickering stove light, Euan approaches the box and kneels. He puts out a hand and rests it on the lid, feeling the warped and cracking paint, cold against his palm. A memory surfaces like a drowned body rising, bloated, to the surface. He inhales sharply, opens the box.

Chocolate bars. Tea bags. Biscuits. Supplies left by kind wanderers. Euan smiles, then closes his eyes and stands. There is a rule: if you take something, you leave something behind. So far, Euan has taken nothing. He comes and goes like a shadow. He shuts the lid, and returns to his stove.

As he eats his pasta, he hears the wind murmur from over the sea, hears the sob of water over sand, hears the door open.

He straightens. 'Hello?'

The stove is out, and the only light is a silver streak from the window. The doorway is in darkness.

'Cold out,' says the stranger. They step into the room, and in the window light, a sea-glow rimes their skin. A man, older than Euan, wearing a long coat. He lowers his hood and moves to the table, sitting beside Euan to remove his boots. His greying hair hangs in lank strands. After he kicks off his boots, he offers a hand to Euan. 'Nick,' he says.

'Euan.'

They shake.

'Colder than a well-digger's arse,' says Nick.

Euan laughs.

'Dram?' Nick reaches into his coat and produces a flask.

'What is it?'

Nick drinks from the flask and sighs. 'Good stuff.' He plants the flask on the table and runs his hands through his hair. In profile, he has a hooked nose, a chin like a crescent moon and heavy-lidded eyes. His skin is wind burnished and red.

Euan takes the flask and offers his bowl of pasta in return. Nick takes it greedily.

They eat and drink in silence, before Euan asks, 'Where you from?'

Nick wipes his mouth. 'North.' He reaches into his pocket and takes out a red woollen cap, pulling it down over his brow.

'Glencoe,' says Euan.

Nick smiles and sets the bowl down on the table with a clank. He takes the flask from Euan and stands, wandering to the window and looking out at the shore. 'Did you see all the debris across the bay? Bottles, glass, rope and such.' He drinks from the flask and sighs. 'It just washes up here. Beautiful sometimes. When the light hits it right. Like a broken mosaic.'

'Hadn't thought of it like that.'

Nick drinks again and tosses the flask to Euan.

Euan catches it and grins. 'My father said sharing a drink with a stranger is a sacred thing.'

'Aye,' says Nick. 'We must look out for each other. There's a code.'

Euan feels warmth radiate through his limbs. He takes off his coat and tucks his hands into his pockets. 'Travelling light?' he says.

Nick raises his eyebrows.

'You've no pack.'

'Got everything in my coat,' says Nick. He turns back to the bay and watches the water. 'Here, let's have a story.'

Euan leans back, smiling at the giddy sensation. He says, 'Part of the code, eh? Getting pished and telling stories.'

'Tell us what brings you here.' Nick's breath fogs the window. The light drifts through in cloudy wraiths.

Euan is quiet. The memory surfaces again.

Nick rubs his woollen cap and says, 'Eh, no worries.' He clears his throat, then walks over to the metal box in the corner, taking out a pack of biscuits. He opens them and eats like a starving man. He punctuates with a mighty burp, then walks to the windowsill and takes out a piece of bone from his pocket. It is whittled into the shape of a small dragon. He places it on the windowsill and meets Euan's eye.

Euan does not know what to make of the man, but there is a sense of knowing between them. A complicity. He likes him. For a while, they talk in the way men do, at the edge of the world; time's eye strays from them and words become weightless. Above the bay, the stars fall into place like cast runes. The men laugh and drink, until Nick says, 'Now, how about that story?'

Euan considers, then sighs and leans forward across the table, facing Nick. 'I'll tell it, if you want to know.'

'I do.'

'Well, I'll trade you. You tell yours after.'

'I will.'

Euan nods. 'Okay then.'

****

She was waiting to be picked up after school. She had stayed late for art club. I remember she told me the teacher kept making them paint apples, but she was bored of that, so she painted giraffes instead. She wouldn't stop going on about giraffes. She wanted one as a pet. She was funny, my sister.

It was winter, and she was wrapped up in her green down jacket. Her hair would pool in the hood. By the time Dad remembered he needed to pick her up, it was dark. The street lamps were on... I keep asking myself why he forgot. Maybe it was the change of schedule; her staying late for art club? He was a single dad, so he always seemed stretched. When he finally realised, it must have been around six, seven. It was only him in the house. I was out.

Dad got in the car and drove. On the road, he tried to phone the school, but no one answered. At a set of traffic lights, he checked if Natasha had sent him any texts. She hadn't. He tried to phone her, but it went straight through to voicemail. She must have been out of battery. Why else wouldn't she pick up?

He sped down the narrow road that led to the school, telling himself she'd be there waiting. Maybe a teacher was with her? The country lanes were winding and dark but rarely used at that time. He went faster. A dread thickened in his throat. She would be waiting. He pictured her, standing by the school gates, nose reddened by the cold, her straw-yellow hair turned grey by the dusk. She would be waiting.

He pulled up to the school gates. No one there. The gates were locked. The lights in the classrooms were all out. He got out the car and searched.

'Natasha!'

Nothing. Only the roosting of rooks and the echo of her name. He waited for three minutes. He got back in the car and phoned a friend whose child went to the same school, asked if they had seen Natasha leave with anyone else. They said, no. They asked if everything was okay. He hung up on them.

He drove around the school, searching the darkness. Figures of lurching men formed from the branches of trees and the shadows under streetlamps. Warmth began to well in his cheeks, he felt tears in his eyes. Blinking, he drove back, scouring the roadside, window lowered, calling her name. How long had she waited for him? Had she been scared?

Recently, another child had gone missing in the area. A boy. He had not been from Natasha's school, but everyone knew. They had found his gloves in the forest.

He decided he would drive home and grab a torch so that he could search the wood around the school; sometimes Natasha would get lost in thought and go wandering. He would call me and ask me to search with him. Driving on, he pulled out his phone. He came to a corner and slammed on the brakes, skidding on the fog-damp road. He drove his foot down on the accelerator and drove away, finding my number, tapping the dial button, bringing it to his ear. It rang.

My voice coming through. 'Dad?'

His eyes rolled back to the road. Too late to do anything. On impact, he flew forward, hit his head on the wheel.

Blood misted the air around the car.

He blinked and saw that green down jacket lying twisted on the road.

****

Nick is quiet. He lays both hands down on the table. He speaks without looking up. 'To lose a family member… Terrible thing.'

Euan sniffs and rubs his nose roughly with a sleeve.

'And in that way… God.'

'Almost funny.' Euan lies back on the bench beside the table.

'You told the story like you were there.'

Euan snorts.

Nick rubs his woollen cap. 'So that's why you're walking?'

Euan crosses his legs and folds his hands behind his head. It's all the reply he gives.

Nick takes up the flask and drains it. He screws the top back on and places it delicately in the centre of the table. The tide fills their silence with its slow pulse.

'So,' says Euan, 'Why don't you tell me?'

'Tell you what?'

Euan sits up. 'You come here alone, won't say where you're from, and you've no pack. What business you have out here?'

Nick's eyes drift up from the table and meet Euan's. He licks his lips, and then slowly smiles. His teeth are like those of an old comb. 'We're bold when we're pished, eh?'

'Only fair. I told you my story.'

'How will you know I'm not lying?'

'I'll know.'

Nick scoffs. 'Will you now?' He rises from the table and wanders around the room for a while. Eventually, he settles by the window, picks up the bone carving and holds it in the moonlight. In that moment, his face begins to drip with water, his clothes are sodden, barnacles rise up through his skin, and the scent of festering seaweed is thick.

Euan blinks and Nick is back to normal. He wonders what was in the flask. He rubs the bridge of his nose and tries to calm his hammering heart.

The carving shimmers.

'You take something, you leave something behind,' Nick says.

'Who…who are you?'

Nick tosses the carving and catches it in a heavy fist. 'There's a code. Who knows when the rules were made? But they're there, and should be followed.'

Euan stares at the man, the sting of seaweed still in his nose. His limbs feel heavy, his head light. Nick's eyes glitter like sunken coins. He speaks.

****

What makes a person wander? Two reasons. The first is that they are searching for something. The second is that they found it already and don't like the answer. My father called it the tread-song. Sometimes a man would pass through our village with that far-away look in his eye and my father would say to me, 'You see that one, he's lost in the tread-song.' When I saw someone like that, I always thought how lonely they must be. But they weren't alone. They had their tread-song. I know that now.

It was a man like this that came to stay at my father's inn. He had with him a daughter. Georgie. They arrived one night, paid for a room, and when the morning came, the man was gone. We found Georgie, alone, weeping. My brother and I peered from behind our father's back as he took up Georgie in his arms and held her until she quieted. We didn't know why her father left. We never knew. Our pa told Georgie that it would all be okay. He would care for her. My brother and I said nothing, we only stared up at the sallow-faced girl, amazed.

Years passed, and Georgie almost forgot about her father, lost to the tread-song. She grew tall, keen-eyed and quick – she had to keep me and my brother at bay. He and I did what brothers do; we squabbled over her, showboating and fawning, scrapping in the dirt while she laughed. I'd always lose the fights and my brother would stand triumphant over me, and then sulk, when Georgie came to my side.

That was the pattern of our days until my brother grew tired. He moved away to the city and left me and Georgie alone. We cared for my father as he died and grief brought us closer. It was natural, the way we fell together, like an answer to a question that had lain dormant in us all our lives.

We looked after the inn, as my father lay dying and our roots drove deeper. My brother returned and stayed at the inn while we arranged the funeral. After Dad was buried, he stayed a little longer, helping us with the business, telling tales about where he had been over the years. He was exciting to listen to; he made you want to run away with him.

No surprise Georgie fell for him. When I found them together, I felt every root I had planted in that earth torn up. Seeing them…I had a choice. Hurt my brother, or leave and seek the tread-song.

I set out, walking until every sinew in me howled. Then, I came to this place. To Camasunary Bay. I lay down on that thrust of rock, just out there. I let the salt-waves lap at my ankles and the seaweed tickle my toes. I fell asleep there, and when I woke, there was a man beside me.

He was an ordinary man. Older than I. A gruff way about him. I told him my story, and he told me his. He said he had come to the bay by boat, and that he was done with it now. He was ready to return home.

After a long time talking, he asked if I wanted his boat. He said it had served him well and would me too. He gestured down the bay and there it was, rocking slowly against the shore. An old barnacled thing, but stout. I took his offer. Sailed out that morning.

As I left the shore, I saw him walking, surefooted, out of the bay.

****

Euan staggers to his feet.

'If you want it, it's yours,' says Nick. He gestures out to the thrust of rock.

Euan moves beside Nick. He looks through the window, out at the bay, and sees the boat. It juts from the thrust like an old stone.

'…Where would I go?'

'Where it takes you.'

Euan turns to face Nick. The old man's breath is cold, like wind through a sea cave. Euan feels it on his cheek. He shivers. Nick is gazing at him, eyes narrowed as if he were following a skimmed stone. A moment of quiet.

'I would not have judged you, had you told the truth,' says Nick.

Euan feels something rise in him like the need to cough. There is heat behind his eyes. He blinks back tears. 'What do you mean?'

Nick steps closer, puts a hand on Euan's shoulder.

The sea stills, the light fades, and there is only the memory of his sister's broken body through the shattered windscreen. His hands still on the wheel, shaking.

Euan finds himself in the arms of Nick. He weeps into the man's shoulder, smells the sea.

Nick says nothing. There is nothing to be said.

By now, the stars are fading, being gathered up one by one, to be cast again. There is a moonlight road stretching from the horizon to the shore. It is singing.

A silent agreement is made. Nick takes up Euan's pack, shoulders it and walks to the door.

Euan puts on his coat and follows Nick out, bracing himself against the cold. They share a look, then part.

Euan walks along the thrust, to the boat. He closes his eyes and listens to the song.

SECOND PLACE

Beacons

Sophie Holland

Lily squats over the pond poking her stick at the frogspawn, a wobble of tiny black jelly-clad commas. On another day they might make Richard think of his pancreas, but Lily is rapt. Her raptness fills him with a glow, like he has swallowed liquid gold. Richard is Lily's father, only a wafer of himself – a slither like a new moon. One day soon he will blow away, a dandelion seed in the breeze. This is how he'd like to tell it to Lily when he has to – that she will see him in the fields, a seed on the breeze, rising, watching over her.

Dandelion is one of the words.

A tiny movement pierces the water's surface and flippers away down into the reedy darkness. She stirs the water with her stick.

'Where's it gone?'

'It's a newt,' he says.

'Newt?' she pouts the word – on her lips, words sparkle.

Newt is another one of the words on the list.

A few months ago, Rich received some crow-black news that has steadily pecked at him. It was around then that something else was bothering him. He'd read about it. Words were dropping out of books, of heads, of use. Becoming obsolete. How could they? Acorn, gone. And Bluebell – the overnight spread of purple, like a tide. Apparently, no one says these words. That can't be true. Conker. Imagine a childhood without Conker? And Starling. And Wren – tiny virtuoso soprano, pluckiest of creatures with its tail pointing at the sun. Wren, for God's sake! He is incensed. Splenetic. Pancreatic. Ha.

He is also galvanised. Words. What you can't say you can't picture, and what you can't picture you can't love. *Lily Lily Lily.* Trapped in her indoor life.

You could say it was an epiphany; the call to fatherhood exploding inside him for the first time, a firework in the chest, almost but not quite too late. Fatherhood, father, Dad. He hasn't been much of one. He hasn't been one at all. Now he knows. He knows that before he goes, he must get his daughter to look up: she needs to know what she won't have words for.

Every month he has looked into the dark eyes in her oval face and thought to himself *Where did you come from?* The answer, of course, is the woman who seduced and discarded him almost twelve years ago. She had chosen him,

Rich the fool, as he might live up to his name. Ha. And because she knew he had no desire for offspring. She kept the child to herself, until the summer of the girl's ninth year, when she decided it was time for Rich to make his appearance.

Once a month, these past two years, Rich and Lily have sat side by side in dark cinemas, across from each other in pizza places, strings of cheese swinging from their lips in lieu of conversation. What did he know of children? Leaky, howling, insatiable, mayhem. And now, stranger still, a poised mini-woman with black-rimmed eyes and sparkling nails; polished, impermeable. How will he get through? Little white stumps of earphones poking from her ears, singing tunelessly, alarmingly, of *sweet slow kisses from my baby,* and always looking down.

On a Saturday in early February, he drives her up to Beacon Hill under a moody sky. Windscreen wipers bat at the drizzle. He glances at her in the passenger seat. She's not come prepared – her shoes resemble ballet slippers, a tiny striped bag sits in her lap covered with inexplicable multicoloured zips.

'Up here there's an awesome view,' he says, his voice bright. Lily nods and unzips a zip, then another, pulls out her earphones.

'Top of the world,' he says, gripping the wheel.

They park near the top. He'd planned a longer walk but he is losing his nerve. They make their small ascent side by side on spiky ground. Mercifully the rain has stopped. He wants to take her hand. He can hear her humming – faint atonal peeps from under her hood. Should he ask about the music? He strides on, he must show her, he *must.* If he could, he would have waited for primroses, the evening scream of swifts, an orange sunset. Instead, they stand beside the thick grey obelisk in tufts of colourless grass, brown fields tumble away in front of them criss-crossed with hedges in dark clumps. Even this evokes a bleak beauty. At the bottom, the city sprawl nestles low against a burgeoning sky. To his left, a line of yew trees scratch their way down the hillside. Two large black birds crouch in the branches. He fills his lungs and looks around, but Lily has strayed from his side. On a flat patch of ground to his right, she's jumping from side to side.

The birds take flight, a sudden spray of black against the lumpy grey. He runs over to join her, ready with his spiel. She's looking down at her feet, practising something.

'They're ravens,' he points and, without meaning to, starts reeling off words. 'Fern, bramble lark – and magpie! We saw one on the way here...' She takes a step backwards as he carries on, his pitch rising. 'And – and heather! I'll find you some.' He scans the ground. What is he thinking? They're not high enough. He looks back at her – she's got her head cocked to one side.

'Heather's in my class,' she says. She takes an earphone out, looks up at the sky, takes the other one out. 'She has to have a special teacher with her.' Rich waves this away as a gust of panic rises in his throat.

'Heather's one of the *words*,' he flings out his arms. 'You need all this! It could save your *life*!'

Her face is blank.

'Words are vanishing, Lily.' His arms drop to his sides and his voice slides back to normal. 'I don't want all this lost to you.'

'What?' she says, wrinkling her nose, 'what words?' He sees her shiver. Any minute now she will stomp off to the car. He longs for her to stay with him here on the hill, to open her eyes in wonder.

'Words to name the world,' he says, – *now* she will understand what's at stake? Lily thinks about this and looks at him, confused.

'Is that what you're sad about?'

'Ah, no. Huh.' What was he saying? It was urgent but it's gone. He stares into her face. Her dark brown eyes look steadily into his, giving nothing of her world away. Brambles knot his thoughts, Lily twirling on the grass just a minute ago. He opens his mouth to a tendril of smoky breath but no words. Feeling winded he squats down, still their eyes are locked. She's taller than him now.

Is that what you're sad about?

He has to look away.

Lily squares her shoulders, raises her chin.

'There's too many words anyway,' she says with authority. What? Rich may have to lie down. Something is being pulled from him, unravelling somewhere.

'And there's always new ones,' Lily says with a shrug.

'New ones,' he repeats. He's lost his grip. Words. He was trying to open her eyes. He pats the ground behind him – too wet to sit.

'Like Hashtag,' Lily says, with her head on one side making him think of a robin. 'Blog,' she switches sides, 'Twitter.'

He reels. He feels like he is balanced on a ledge, he mustn't look down. His knees are hurting in this squat.

'What I wanted,' he starts slowly, putting a hand on the ground in front to steady him, 'was for you to –' But Lily's not listening. She's heading back down the hill, away from him. His heart is so heavy it might grind them both to a halt. With great effort, Rich unfurls himself to standing and heads after her.

Almost at the car, he finds her hunkered down, swiping at the ground, picking something.

She swipes again, turns, and shows him a clutch of pointy green leaves.

'For next door's rabbit,' she says. With her free hand she rips another handful and holds up two fistfuls. 'He *loves* dandelions.'

Inside his chest hope flaps in great beats, like a heron rising from a lake.

After he takes Lily home, he goes to his friend's cottage by the sea. Standing on the rocks he allows himself to be hypnotised by the swish and suck, the raking crackle of the tide going out, peels of scattered spume falling in a heartbeat to calm. He understands he is the sea –inside his chest rage builds, roars, spits, then drops away. *There's too many words anyway.* He smiles now at the wisdom in this, in spite of the grammar. Yet on his slow walk back to the cottage, salt in his nostrils, his own new words jab at him in sharp pricks: ductal, histopathology, metastasize. Palliative.

The month passes. They sit across from each other at his kitchen table, he taps at his laptop for inspiration, she swipes her small pink-cased screen as the day crouches at the window, dank and mocking.

Bingo. He turns the laptop to face her. She looks up from her phone.

'Smoke,' she says, unimpressed. He shakes his head.

'Birds,' he says, nodding at the screen, making an upward spiral motion with his finger. She leans in.

'It's smoke,' she says. 'What's burning?'

He laughs, 'Seriously, it's starlings, thousands of them. I've seen them do it.'

'If you say so.' She goes back to her phone. He feels like a squashed bug. He leaves a long pause.

'What would *you* like to do?' he says finally, trying to keep his voice level, free of his creeping desperation. Then, like the jewel-flash of a kingfisher, an idea swoops in. He slaps both palms on the table.

'Let's go to the sea.'

She looks confused, 'On *holiday*?'

'No, the *ocean,* cliffs, wind in your hair –'

She curls her hair around her index finger, a sparkle of blue pokes through on the tip.

'Come on,' he says.

Lily picks her way like a careful stick insect down the knobbly path, mud and stones flanked by a high hedge either side. The short walk takes forever. When the hedge drops away, they're battered by the wind. And there is it, the March sea, wide and grey and seething. A gull, like a small plane sweeps by, too close, Lily stumbles back, shrieks.

'Come on!'

She grips his fingers as he leads her further out. They pick over the rocks together and stop at the furthest point.

'Look!' he points at a gannet bobbing in the froth. Lily follows his gaze, the bird dips down and vanishes. The sky brightens a shade as the sun pushes at the cloud.

'... going to die?' Lily shouts. He jerks his head towards her. She says something else but the wind snatches her words.

Is she asking him?

A crag of silver outlines the cloud, like lightning, and disappears. Rich can't decide where to look or what to say. The gannet pops up again. He's about to point it out when a lazy wave crawls up onto the rock and over Lily's feet. She squeals, looks murderously at the sea, at her shoes. She retreats at a run, away from the lapping enemy.

'They're soaked!' she cries from a flat rock, 'suede's not supposed to get *wet*!' With the last shrill word, the wind whips her hair right over her face. She squats down on the rock hugging her knees. She might be crying. He goes to her side and kneels beside her.

'The sea's a menace, isn't it?' He sits right beside her so she can lean on him. She doesn't move away. 'It's full of treasure though.'

She gives him a stern look and sniffs.

'I used to swim in this, you know,' he says, remembering with a jolt of grief the tingling zing of his skin, like an alarm on the outside of the body.

'In winter?' she says, wide-eyed.

'In winter,' he says, then adds, 'in a wetsuit.' He thinks how alien his life must seem to her.

'What kind of treasure?' she says, rubbing at her shoes with her sleeve.

'Everything you can imagine. I was thinking of the wildlife kind.' He checks he hasn't lost her here, but she's waiting. 'Somewhere in the ocean there's a fish that can give itself a sex-change. It goes under a rock male, and...ta-da! comes out female.'

'No way!' Her mouth drops open, he can see her back teeth.

'Fact,' he says, 'I saw it on a documentary.' Lily takes this in, nods to herself.

'At least it comes out a *girl*,' she says, with a sly smile.

'Ha! At least. That is indeed a bonus.' They look at each other, both with something on the tips of their tongues. The wind drops. Lily picks up a pebble and taps it on the rock, leaving little chalk marks.

'I've got two fish,' she mumbles to the rock. Rich thinks he may have imagined it.

'Wibble and Wobble. I know they're crap names.' She scratches a 'W' carelessly, flicking at the stone. 'Only goldfish. Mum's boyfriend won them at Downsfest. I keep hoping they'll die so I can get better ones.' Rich watches creases form on her brow.

'We could bring them here,' he says, then with a grin, 'feed them to the gannets.'

She puts her hand over her mouth to cover a smile. It is all he can do to stop himself lunging towards her with open arms. He keeps talking.

'Stick them in a plastic bag, filled with water –'

'Or a Tupperware,' Lily says.

'Tupperware, genius!' he almost bellows. 'Ha! They won't know anything, they're not the brightest.'

‘They might like it better,’ Lily says. ‘More space.’

‘They might,’ his throat is thick, his heart sings. He looks at his daughter. ‘They might like it better.’

The sea churns in front of them, all the way to the horizon.

The air grows warmer, reaching towards spring. He pleads for an overnight contact, is staggered that Lily agrees. She must know something. He pitches the tent, though they may not sleep in it – he’ll take her home if she changes her mind. They lie on their backs and gaze up at the winking ink-black sky.

‘All the way out there, all the iron in your blood, that’s where it was made.’

‘Stop telling me things,’ she says.

‘Sorry.’

‘Shhh,’ she says, ‘I’m looking.’ Then after a short while, ‘I’m freezing.’

It clouds over, they light a fire and stare into the leaping flames.

‘What did you want to be?’ she asks.

‘Hmm?’

‘When you were eleven,’ she says ‘what did you want to *be*?’ Her face flickers pink and orange. A thrill shoots through him; she really wants to know. Then a tumbling panic. The answer is forensic pathologist. He won’t speak here of dead bodies, of scraping under fingernails. He needs something poetic, impressive.

‘An inventor,’ he says. She looks back at the fire. A spark jumps out and lands beside her foot, they stare at it as it pulses and fades.

‘I wanted to invent a time machine,’ he says, believing it now himself.

‘I think someone’s already doing that,’ Lily says. Ludicrously, he is put out.

‘Who?’ he scowls.

‘Someone at Nasa,’ she says. ‘I want to be a choreographer but Vanessa says I won’t make it because I’m still not on points. Basically, I only want to do Street and Rockjam though, so it doesn’t matter.’

This huge, incomprehensible speech is sublime to him. Vanessa’s clearly a fuckwit.

‘You’ll be a fantastic choreographer,’ he says, wishing he was young and hip.

Lily shrugs. ‘I don’t think Dance is on the options at Moorland Green anyway.’

‘Dance is always an option,’ he says. A whispery hoot comes from the woods. He cocks his head to listen. Lily doesn’t notice, she stands up to fumble in her pockets and pops her earphones in. The fire crackles, another breathy hoot. He checks to see if Lily’s heard it, but she’s bobbing her head to her own music, eyes on the dwindling flames. He’ll take her to the pond next, there might be tadpoles.

He leans in to place another log, savours the heat, almost burning his face and warm across his chest. She mouths words he can't make out, her face flickering pink. Her shoulders start to rise in small rhythmic movements: left shrug, right shrug, left, right. Now she lifts her legs a fraction, one at a time, now her arms fan out and she makes a wave with her whole body. He's careful to keep his eyes on the fire and watches her from the corners. She doesn't seem to mind him being there while she dances.

Shrug, shrug, step, step, arms wide, wave.

It is just the two of them in the corner of a field, a tiny glow in the night. Another hoot comes from the woods. Calling to him. Them. His whole life is here; flapping, sweet, perilous.

THIRD PLACE

The Life and Times of Sam the Wanderer as the End of Days Approaches

Anya Christiansen

I have never lived in a world before The Dogs. Rudie says that means I missed out on *certain meaningful, formative moments in my childhood* and that means that I'm *very different* to her and Elijah. Rudie tells me about all these things I should miss, like *orange juice* and *toothpaste* and *cooked lobster* and *converse shoes* and *comfy bathrobes* and *driving* and *showers* and *McDonald's*. She describes them utterly and completely, in every detail, backwards and forwards. I always smile at her and laugh when she laughs, and tell her I want to hear more about the things she misses.

It's only half of a lie. Because I do want to hear, but only to make Rudie happy.

Elijah never tells me about the things he misses, which is fine. He's just quiet and sits in the corner most of the time. Rudie calls him *brooding.* She says that means 'someone thinking until it makes them sad'.

Rudie says there are lots of things in the world that can make you sad. I don't really get sad. Not like Rudie or Elijah get sad.

Rudie says another reason why Elijah is always sitting in the corner is that he's scared. Rudie says that being scared works kind of like being sad if you're brooding. He holds our gun in his right hand and strokes the cold metal with his left, playing with the bolt handle, slowly assembling and disassembling. His eyes have absorbed its coldness, its sheen, its *impenetrability.* He is a brooding man.

The Dogs are the only things that scare me.

Elijah and Rudie and I sit in a dead person's house, miles and miles away from Rudie's Home, which is somehow different from a house. I haven't figured out why they're different yet. It's been days since we've gone anywhere because Rudie and Elijah knew there was a Horde coming. When a Horde comes, we have to stay inside.

Sometimes, Rudie will hold a piece of paper – a map – close to her face, as the light shines in from the gaps between the planks on the windows. She drags her fingers along the paper and counts the numbers that tell her where we are in the world. She gives some spots funny names, like *Wellington* or *Nelson*, and tells me what they were like before.

The last name Rudie told me was Papakura. That's where we are now. It's a place of desertedness. No animals, no trees and shadows everywhere. I think that's the way all named places are. Big blocks of grey, or sometimes boxes covered with colourful words like *pharmacy* and *cafe* and *takeaway.*

Rudie leads us to them on things she calls *motorways* that people didn't always walk on and that weren't always crumbly and bursting with weeds. Rudie says they're the way people find things. I don't think she's right.

I find things through a never-ending stream of moments. I see it in clouds, signs and sunsets. I remember the curve of the land as it rushes up to greet me; the colour of the sky and the way the wind picks through my hair. I see it in the bend of a corner and the shape of the trees. And then I know where I am and where everything else is around me. I'm very different though because I don't know the world before The Dogs.

I can't help being different. It's all I can think about when Rudie tells me about the *malls* and the *restaurants* and the *supermarkets*. Rudie'll be telling me a story and I'll lean on her shoulder. She'll brush her fingers through my hair, and I'll close my eyes. I'll take every word I don't know and invent a world where they're something new. They're the sounds that the birds make that echo in the cold and the quiet. They're the way the light hits Rudie's face when the sun just touches the horizon. They're the smiles that tug at the edge of Elijah's mouth when I give him a leaf or a flower from the veins and arteries of the broken motorway we walk.

I would never tell Rudie the way I find things. It's the sort of thing that makes Rudie sad.

There are countless things in Rudie's universe, and she misses every single one of them. She misses all the small things and the big things and the things I think are probably useless because we live fine without them. She always tells me how much we took it all for granted and how much harder the world is without them. Sometimes she'll cry then, just a little bit, and then we'll think about something else.

Sometimes we find the things Rudie talks about. They're usually in one of the boxes people have left behind for us inside of their basements. Rudie's always so happy then and sometimes even Elijah will smile and hug me. It was days and days and days ago that we found *toothpaste* which was probably the last new thing we found.

Toothpaste is this sparkly, sticky stuff that people used to put in their mouth to clean their insides. Rudie says it's for teeth, but you don't even need to clean your teeth. It contains *stardust* and other stuff like *apple seeds* and *elephant tears*. Or big words like that at least. Toothpaste is blue like oceans or rivers or Rudie's pants. Rudie tells me they're the same thing. The same colour. Even though I've seen a river before and I've seen bits of the sea, and they're not. She says before The Dogs they used to be different. Blue, not red and grey and brown.

It's really weird and sticky and cold. The toothpaste I mean. I stuck some in my mouth when Rudie and Elijah weren't looking, and it burnt my tongue, but in a cold way. I smelt like toothpaste for forever after that. I don't know why anyone would eat it. But I'm very different. I've never lived in a world before The Dogs.

When we're stuck in a basement for days and days, we always come back to The Dogs. They haunt us even when we can't see them. When Rudie is done talking about the world to me, and I've done all the schoolwork she can think of, we always come back to The Dogs.

The Dogs came in the night, cloaked in shimmering shadows, howling and baying in the dark. They had teeth the size of arms and arms the size of me and they had eyes that made you want to melt right into the ground, huge and glowy-yellow in the night. It's all you can see of them when they come out of the darkness.

Rudie always says it's a miracle that she survived. She didn't have any planks on the windows and doors as we do now. She was all alone in her house when she heard the sound of the Horde. I know that sound like the back of my hand. It's the sound of a thousand howls in the dark, the sniffling and growling that pricks up the hair on your arms and legs. That feeling of their hot breath on your neck. So Rudie grabbed her cow prod and her hunting rifle and locked every door in the house, keeping herself hidden in her bedroom. She said they came inside and sniffed at everything; knocking things over, breaking her tables and her beds, eating all of her food. She waited up all night until she couldn't hear them anymore. Rudie says she watched as the sun rose for the first time in the days After The Dogs and that she followed that sun until she found me.

Sometimes I can tell when Rudie is lying. I think that she followed the sun for a long time before she found me.

'Oi, Sam.' Rudie whispers. She's at the door, her eye to the hole in the board. 'It's time to go.'

I stand up slowly. Until a couple of months ago I was the same height as her. Now we're nowhere close. I'm taller than Elijah too, so much taller he calls me *abnormal.* It makes the world look so different. I'm *very* different though so I'm used to it.

Elijah stands up too. He's very skinny, and his skin hugs his bones. Shadows cut deep underneath his cheekbones, and his eyes have sunken into his face like a boot does in the snow. He's got hair that's thin and dark grey and hangs like spider webs around his face. He puts on his jacket and zips it up, but his hand never lets go of the rifle. Shoes, socks, and then he slings the rifle over his shoulder.

Elijah's story is different from Rudie's. Rudie says Elijah will *never be the same again.*

Before The Dogs, Elijah had a wife. A wife was a person you promised you were going to live your whole life with and make a family and have kids. Elijah did that, and he was happy.

Then The Dogs came.

Elijah has insomnia which means he can't sleep very well, so he was up when they came. He was in the bathroom, in the shower. His wife was in the bedroom. The kids were down the hall, sleeping like *little angels.* I didn't know what an angel is but Rudie says that's not important.

'And well... No one can escape from The Dogs once they find you.'

Elijah always says it that way. And he never says any more.

Sometimes he won't for a couple of days.

There was a woman, Elijah and Rudie knew before, who was my *mother.* She died. Then it was just me and Elijah and Rudie forever after.

I go over to help Elijah with the boards that block the door. We work methodically, in sync like we always have. Rudie does the windows.

One time I snuck Rudie's paper from her when she and Elijah left me alone one night. I stared at it for a long time, trying to make sense of the wiggly lines and the greens and blues. It didn't feel as special as I thought it would to drag my finger across the paper or pronounce the impossibly small words that covered the map. She had circled special names – Auckland and Invercargill. Invercargill's Rudie's Home. I know that. Sometimes Rudie will talk about it. But more than Invercargill, they talk about Auckland. It's our destination. They're both sure we'll find what they left behind there: big piles of *orange juice* and *toothpaste* and everything else they had before The Dogs, like *happiness* and *love.*

I don't mind us not being in Auckland. Auckland is a named place – and like the rest, it will be a land of desertedness. I know this, but it's something I wouldn't tell Rudie. Or Elijah. They would both become brooding. I've thought about this.

Still, I can't stop wishing that they would let us live somewhere out in the unnamed places – maybe at Rudie's Home or Elijah's Home. I'll hunt for them because I'm good at that and they can garden and write down all of their stories and leave it there for some other Sam, Elijah and Rudie to find.

I pry off the final plank and let it fall to the floor with a *clunk.* Elijah wrenches the door open, releasing a shower of dust. There, the outside waits.

The street is destroyed. The concrete has turned to rubble. Some of the tall grey boxes have fallen in the distance. But the dust is clearing.

Rudie walks out of the house and moves her hand across the scratches that cover the walls.

'They're getting stronger,' she says. Elijah comes out of the house, shielding his eyes from the sun.

'We had better keep moving then,' Rudie says. She and Elijah begin to walk along the road, jumping between the bits of concrete that are left.

I stay a moment, looking and listening. The bird calls echo across the world, and slowly but surely the sun begins to rise. It touches my skin like *little angels*.

Broken Blood

Pauline Plummer

Daniyal looks through an open doorway and sees a goat tethered and children playing. Two women are rolling out rotis. Another is fanning charcoal into fire. An old man with a white beard sits on a cane chair, telling his beads.

****

He walked through the garden and looked around. The first white heads of snowdrops began the year and now, in summer, the beds were a profusion of agapanthus, orange crocosomia and firework azaleas. He lifted the tag on a blue poppy from Tibet and his knee knocked a fern from Gough Island, with drops of dew along its stems. Sometimes the tags blew off in the storms, and it was impossible to remember the names and countries they had been brought from, by his father and then, latterly, by him. The air was moist and dripping, humming with the flight of bees and butterflies, demoiselles and dragonflies from the pond.

A breeze off the Irish Sea banged the shutters on the old house. Daniyal walked past the pond, thick with lilies and pitcher plants. Patches of blue sky reflected in the water. He stood and looked. In December, on a night of freezing fog, he had seen what he thought was a shape of her or a sense of her. He closed his eyes. He could just about remember his child's hand in his mother's, cool and light.

'Are you coming in for your breakfast, Dan?' His father's voice, loud and clipped, cut through the garden. He made his way in and took his coffee and warm bread rolls onto the shaky veranda.

'Have you got all your documents in a safe place?'

'Everything's sorted, Dad.'

The old tabby cat wound through the slots in the veranda. He was there to keep mice out, but the day before he'd brought in a thrush. Daniyal could have wept.

His father joined him on the veranda. 'I'll drive you to Swansea and you can get the train to London from there.'

'Thanks. Maia is meeting me at Heathrow.'

'Maia.' His father slammed the door as he went inside. Daniyal didn't know if it was anger or emotion. Was there no way father and daughter would ever speak to each other again? His sister remembered growing up here as if shadowed by a canopy thick with unanswered questions.

He tried to remember what he saw on the pond, the shadowy shape, beckoning him. He couldn't think of her in traditional clothes. All the photos that were hidden, but which he had found, showed her wearing jeans and blouses, of the two children with her in the garden, or playing on the beach, at the foot of the cliffs, laughing as she splashed them.

Daniyal twisted the sign on the entrance to the gardens to *Closed.* His father, Marshall, took the coast road to Haverfordwest. They glimpsed the blue-green of sea, in gaps between the hills. Daniyal studied his father's craggy profile. 'Any advice about travelling in Kashmir?' he asked.

There was a long silence, as his father negotiated a roundabout and slipped onto the fast road to Swansea. 'Choose a guide you trust, use your instinct. The menfolk won't like it if you're too friendly to any women you meet. You don't need trouble.' He made a noise that was half a chuckle and half a grunt. 'And don't fall in love with a Kashmiri woman.'

The crowds and noise in Heathrow overwhelmed Daniyal. The gleaming racks of bottles and the cloying smell of perfumes, mixed with pizza, beer and sushi, made him nauseous.

'Dan.' Maia's voice was in his ear, her hand on his arm, her olive face with its thick black brows and lashes looking into his. Her blackberry hair had been pulled into a tight bun so that it stretched the skin on her forehead.

Over coffee, he told her about the endangered plants he was going to collect and about the journey into the valleys of Kashmir. She pulled an ordnance survey map from her handbag and unfolded it. 'I've been researching the area. There must be members of our family, our mother's family, the Kathwari, there.' She pointed to the rectangles of houses of a village in the mountains. 'Will you go there Dan, please?'

He bent close to the map. How would this connect with his route? The village was close to the border and this could be dangerous, but he wouldn't stand out like a white man would. 'Maybe, Maia. Let me see how it goes.' He put his arm around her shoulders. 'You haven't asked about Dad.'

Her black eyes became sharpened obsidian. 'I see he's let you grow your hair below your collar? Loosening the military rules, is he? If you grew a beard, you'd fit in even more.'

'I've been having those dreams again,' he said.

'She comes to you but not to me.'

He put his hand on hers.

She turned away from him. 'We only have his version of what happened.'

He looked at her frowning face. There was no placating her bitterness for growing up in that creaking, motherless house, and the exotic garden she grew to hate. She kissed him on the cheek and he moved into the security section.

****

Daniyal rests a night in a hotel in Islamabad, before taking the bus to Muzaffarabat in Kashmir. Despite the winding and precipitous roads, he is enchanted by the landscape of mountains cutting down to river valleys and scattered villages. He catches a glimpse of distant, snow-covered peaks in a wash of pink, dusk light. Other passengers try to speak to him in their language but he knows only a few words. They share their roti and chicken with him. He shows them photographs of the plants he wants to collect and tries to explain that they are endangered, but they smile, not understanding why a grown man would be travelling with such photos. The gaily decorated bus careers round hairpin bends. At the border, a guard with a fierce moustache questions him. He takes his British passport away, to show to an officer. The guard examines his books and photographs, and Daniyal wonders how much of the English he understands. Perhaps they think he's a spy.

'My mother was from Kashmir,' he says. 'Her name was Kathwari. Her family live in Sharda in the Neelum Valley.'

'But you don't speak our language.'

'No, my English father looked after us. My mother drowned.'

The officer pulls at his moustache and examines the equipment, lifting plastic containers to the light, searching through the tools.

Daniyal knows this journey is not without risk but he will blend in with Kashmiri people, with his light brown skin, dark hair and eyes. He decides to buy some local clothes as soon as possible. Perhaps he is coming home. He has never felt as if he completely belonged in Pembrokeshire. The days of name-calling were a long time ago, mainly in school, but that word, *Paki*, has left its echoes. The Qureshi boys and he were the only Asian children in the school. And then he was an outsider, with a tragedy trailing in his wake, like the slime left by a slug.

They let him through and the bus continues to the capital city. At UNESCO headquarters, he meets his guide. Rizwan will take him into the mountains to collect medicinal plants and rare orchids. His English is good and he seems enthusiastic and knowledgeable. He has a thick beard and, under his waterproof jacket, wears traditional kurta and suthan in mustard coloured cotton. They discuss the areas to search, including the Lachi Khan Forest. The Land Rover and driver will arrive in the morning but Daniyal is restless and cannot sleep. He goes out onto the veranda and breathes in pine resin blowing in from the forest, the earth wet from the afternoon's rain, the scent of wood-smoke from cooking fires.

Rizwan is happy to detour to the east of the valley, to reconnect Daniyal with his roots. He asks Daniyal why he has no knowledge of his mother's family. Daniyal does not know. He has no photos or information about cousins, or aunts and uncles. Was there some terrible falling out? Was it his father? He can be so unreasonable, so full of anger. For the first time, he wonders whether there is a story here, which may be difficult for people to talk about. I have been too passive, he thinks, too unquestioning but now I must find out. The compulsion he feels pushes him. It is his mother's birthday in August, and he wants to be there, in Sharda.

The driver drops them in the village the next day and by asking around, they find a Kathwari compound. Rizwan enters the courtyard and explains to the women working there who Daniyal is; they look up from their cooking and point to where he leans in the doorway. An older woman, with a brightly patterned scarf loose over her hair, beats her breast, as if in a state of shock and beckons him into the courtyard. An old man with a white beard, sat in a cane chair, telling his beads, does not move.

Through Rizwan this woman, who is his mother's older sister, talks. Tabina, his mother, was always laughing as a child, mischievous and plump, but clever at school. Their father had sent her to college and she worked in an office for an NGO that was developing agriculture in the area. 'Mr Marshall was working here. We did not know he was a British soldier. We thought he was working for the NGO. Tabina had loved a boy before, but our father did not approve of him and did not allow them to marry. She was a very emotional person. A neighbour saw her alone in a car with this Mr Marshall. He was older than her and they were embracing. Our father was very angry and locked her in a room, but she broke the window and ran away. Mr Marshall took her back to England. If they had stayed here, they might have been killed. She phoned me sometimes from England.'

She passes the palm of her hand lightly around Daniyal's face. 'You have the shape of her face,' she says, 'wide, open-eyed. I could only speak to her on the phone when I was alone. The family wanted no contact with her. She told me she missed her home, that her husband was cruel and cold. She told me about the birth of your sister and was sometimes crying, saying, *what have I done*? His aunt lowers herself onto a chair and wipes her face with her scarf. 'Then all those years of silence when she has not made contact.'

'She seems to think she has told you too much,' said Rizwan, when he finished translating.

'There was no body found, my father told me,' Daniyal says. 'The sea took her.' He doesn't tell her that Marshall gave the cause of her death as suicide. He knows this is a terrible sin in Islam and they will believe she has been sent to hell. His aunt puts her hands on her head and sobs wrack her body until her scarf falls off. Daniyal picks it up and drapes it over her shoulder. He tells her that he sees his mother in dreams and that she stands, her clothes dripping, with her head bent.

'She wants to tell you something,' says his aunt, between sobs.

He stays the night, sleeping in a room with some cousins. They fuss over him, this English man who looks like them but understands nothing. Since they are still at school, they practise their English, asking about football teams and which he prefers, Man U or Man City? Daniyal shakes his head. He doesn't know anything about football or even cricket.

The mattress is hard. Through the window, he can see torn scraps of clouds blowing in front of the moon. The feeling of being here, where his mother grew and lived her life, is so powerful he cannot sleep. He closes his eyes and concentrates on the sounds and smells of the house; he rubs his hands across the rough, whitewashed wall. In a day or so, he will set off to the slopes of the mountains in the North, to do his work, leaving these people who are family. Does he belong here more than in Wales? He sees his mother in his aunt, the same gestures and tone of voice. He is nervous around the menfolk, who seem stern and suspicious. They were angry with his mother so perhaps they think that he also is unclean.

He gets up quietly and walks outside. A chained guard dog barks. There is a chill in the air but he walks down the path to the river, past other wooden houses. The stars are brilliant and flickering and he can see the smear of Milky Way across the sky. He disturbs geese on his way to the swiftly flowing river, pounding over boulders, torrents from the mountains.

He thinks of his bitter sister, as if her pain will never be healed. And he, who remembers their mother more clearly, wonders how she could have left them and walked into the blue- green waves. Their father's regime was strict and responsible. *We had lots of lists and learning, but no hugs and so little laughter. But we were safe, weren't we?*

He sees a shimmering shape over the water. At first, he imagines it as a pale scarf carried in the wind. He slips out of his trainers and walks over the stones. The water round his ankles is icy. If he can only reach her. The water is inky, with little pieces of moon in the eddies. The hem of his kurta is now sodden and pulled at by the water.

'Mother,' he shouts above the roar of water. He thinks he sees a blurred shape. It disappears. If he goes further he'll be sucked into the current. He stands, shivering and sobbing. *Why does she come to him?* He thinks of his aunt's words.

In the morning, over tea, he tells Rizwan about his visit to the river. They tear off pieces of warm flatbread, spread with melting butter. Rizwan seems to understand why a soul might be so restless.

'What unhappiness did she have in her life?' he asks.

'I don't know.'

'It is a terrible sin in our religion. If she was in hell would she be visiting like this? Are you sure your father told you everything?'

'No,' says Daniyal. 'My father doesn't do emotions. My sister used to say that my mother must have run away. But that cannot be. She visits me from the spirit world.'

He spends the next day exploring the hills and forests around the village. He brings back wood for his aunt. She gives him an axe and he stacks the pieces onto the pile next to the kitchen, where she is rolling out roti on a round stone. The motion brings back memories of his mother and the taste of warm roti. He bends his head and his aunt lifts it, calling for Rizwan to translate, but telling him to swear he will say nothing to any of the men in the house.

There is something she needs to tell Daniyal. She has been wondering why her sister's soul is so unquiet. 'One time, your mother telephoned and told me there was another man who loved her and she loved him. He was a Muslim like her. 'Oh, Tabina,' I said, 'this is adultery. You must stop this. She never called me again.' She shakes her head, a little, after saying these words, then flicks her scarf over her shoulder and goes back to the kitchen to prepare the evening meal.

Daniyal walks down to the river and throws stones hard into the racing water. It is possible, he thinks, that his sister is right and she ran away. There is another possibility taking shape, a shape that leaves a bitter and poisonous taste in his mouth.

Her Unused Smile

Sarah Dawson

'Am I your master's first choice?' The big-boned woman in magnificent claret and gold stares at the stone floor, twisting the largest of her ruby rings with restless fingers.

The artist's brush almost slithers from his hand. He shoots a 'help me' look at the envoy who'd accompanied him here from England. But the grey-bearded cleric who'd so expertly navigated the difficult path for this portrait – persuading her family it was not immodest for an unwed woman of four-and-twenty to appear unveiled – is attending to the woman's mother. She has not ceased talking since they entered. The pair sit, heads bowed close together, in the far corner of the chamber.

His eyes return to the daughter – who continues to stare at the floor. He should tell her a gentle, but clear, 'no'. If this were art, he would not flinch. Delivering truth is what he is known for; why his portraits are more in demand than any other in his adopted land. But who could hear such an answer and not feel diminished? Certainly, she must never know how many prospective brides have been considered before her (at least nine). Though rumour must have reached her, surely? His master had asked the king of France to send his most eligible relatives to Calais so that he might take his pick, and King Francis's outraged response, 'I am no horse trader!', has become famous.

At least it has at the English court.

Though caution dictates that there it must be whispered.

He is glad that her eyes are still downturned when he says, 'You are all he thinks of now, my lady.'

He watches her as she flashes a hopeful look at her mother. But the dowager is expounding her favourite subjects to her audience of one: 'The Holy Father says...My beloved daughters need…' The man's shoulders have a slumped aspect but he continues to give his full diplomatic attention.

The artist and the woman are as good as alone. Suddenly, she leans towards him. 'Why, then, does your master also request a likeness of my sister?'

'It is, er, customary to take other family likenesses.'

She looks at him steadily – and this time, though heat rises through him, he meets her gaze. He takes in her every feature: the not-so-small nose, the slightly hooded eyes and the mild curve of her mouth. He likes that curve; it softens her face. He longs to see her smile – just for the interest of the thing. But with her father buried only a year past, and her joyless brother now in his place and said to be under their mother's thumb, he supposes there is little to smile about. It is a loss, he thinks, when a person's smile goes unused.

She is taller than his master's previous wives. But that need not be an obstacle. His master had admired the statuesque Madame de Longueville – until she dashed his hopes by saying, 'I may be big in person, but my neck is small'.

Yet another choice rebuff for his court to whisper.

The artist had painted other ladies of stature but one, in particular, had put the rest (truly) in the shade. The widowed Duchess of Milan was a mere sixteen years when he was sent to capture her likeness. He had spent three hours with her, and his coloured sketch – no time for painting: 'I need to see her, Hans' – had sent his master into transports. He had bidden his musicians play their instruments all day long straight after.

If only her rank had not made her as unreachable as the moon – as well as the little matter of his being married already – the artist would have pleaded his own suit. As it was, those three hours they spent together seemed almost to vanish before they had begun. They had conversed in his native German and he had discovered – and hugely admired – her fluency in multiple languages and passion for riding and hunting (as well as the dimples in her cheeks and chin whenever she chanced to smile). Apart from her sable cloak-trim and fine white collar with matching cuffs, she was dressed entirely in black. But such a woman, with her exquisite hands and rosebud mouth, needed no ornament. What she did need – in her words – was 'a second head', if she were to put it at his master's disposal.

He was not sorry that England's hopes were dashed yet again – or that her words, like those of her predecessors, spread through the court with wildfire speed.

It troubled him, seriously, that a portrait of his might lead to a disastrous union. If a lady's father or, in the case of the one before him, her brother, deemed a marital alliance desirable they would have trouble resisting. (He'd wondered sometimes if Renée de Guise, sister of Louise, whose likeness he had also taken, had only sought the religious life when she heard of his master's interest in her.) But he is well paid for these European excursions. Last year he'd received a bonus of ten pounds, above his thirty-pound wage. An artist has to live…

'Is he still grieving for…' The lady hesitates – as if naming the wife she might replace were bad taste or possibly bad luck.

The artist shifts his eyes reluctantly from the drape of her velvet sleeve. 'It is nigh on two years since England was bereaved. My master was devoted to the late queen but now desires to be wed again.'

He blinks at the smoothness of his own reply.

'I suppose he was devoted to his *former* queens once.'

This time his brush clatters to the floor. Dark red tempera spatters the grey stone. He stoops to mop it with a rag, but cannot remove the spreading stain. He frowns as he straightens. 'Alas, neither lady was what she appeared at first.' His linen shirt under his doublet and jerkin instantly prickles. The palace in Düren, capital of this Rhineland dukedom, is warmer than any in London. But it is not merely the August heat here that has suddenly become oppressive. He barely knew his master's first queen, but the second had been a generous patron who had commended him widely. It is a little over three years since her head was sliced from her body by a swordsman from Calais – at the behest of his master. Those words he'd just damned her with he does not believe. That she committed adultery, least of all with her own brother, were charges concocted to make way for a new wife, who might provide his master with a male heir. And be a fresh companion in his bed.

'Did you take their likenesses also?'

He swallows. 'Of one. But the painting was destroyed.'

She is looking at him intently – as if she suspects him of harbouring secrets. Perhaps he has misjudged her. For his secrets are legion. It is not just the second queen he mourns. Another patron, his first in England, was also killed by his master. At least the man he now calls his patron – who also serves this ruthless master – is too highly esteemed to be disposable. The thought revives him. 'I painted the late queen several times. Like you, she favoured red and gold.' He smiles, though it is a courtier's smile. For he will never own how interminable he found those sittings. Or that a proverb of Solomon had played in his head throughout: *There is gold, and a multitude of rubies: but the lips of knowledge are a precious jewel*. The late queen had dressed exquisitely, but shown little learning and no wit, unlike her cultured predecessor. It had struck him, forcibly, that the shape of her mouth reflected this; they could never be called lips of knowledge, so he'd reproduced their lemon-sucking primness. He had been fortunate – he knew he had – that no one had recognised his scriptural hint of a meanness in Queen Jane's understanding. She was, after all, the queen his master still mourned, being mother to his single male heir.

But returning to the lady before him: what hints should he give of what lies beyond her surface? For he is haunted by his master's words 'By God, I trust no one but myself. The thing touches me too near.' He must deliver an exact likeness that conveys also her essence – or suffer the consequences. Fortunately, unlike any sitter before her, the lady has granted him unlimited time – which is generous – and he has now completed his preparatory sketches, in chalk and ink, and moved on to this final tempera painting on parchment. His grey-bearded companion, still a captive audience of the dowager, thinks the lady patently unsuitable (never mind her essence) and has said so in writing: *Although she can read and write in her own language, she has no French, no Latin nor any language besides German; likewise no singing nor playing of any instrument, for they take it here in Germany for a rebuke and an occasion of lightness that great ladies should be learned or have any knowledge of music...*

The artist's patron, however, champions the match. He believes she will soon learn to be different and, more importantly, beget further heirs.

England, he insists, needs a political alliance that will reduce its isolation. The problem has reached a new pitch of urgency since the French king and the Holy Roman Emperor forged a treaty, followed by the Pope taking it upon himself to reissue his bull of excommunication against his master. However, an arranged marriage will –

'This is his first arranged marriage, is it not? Do you think a man can be devoted to his wife when his marriage is arranged?'

Can she discern his thoughts now? He frowns. Coughs. 'My master's first marriage was also arranged – to his brother's young widow – and endured 24 years.' He instantly regrets e*ndured.*

'Not all of them happy.'

Where does she get such acuity without learning? Would it be unseemly to speak of his own marriage, arranged by his father? He has, after all, provided magnificently for his wife and children: Elsbeth was widowed when they wed, with one son already, to which have they have now added Philipp, Katharina, Jakob and Küngold. There have been no bailiffs calling, as in his own childhood, no uncle suing for thirty-four florins. On the contrary, he has added to his wife's wealth, the tannery and dowry she brought with her. But – his eyes return to the stain on the floor – he has been absent for most of his children's growing-up years and he has taken mistresses. The only family portrait he ever painted showed Elsbeth as unutterably weary and his children, likewise, joyless. He had been gone a mere two years then. He has been away many more since. He had wanted to show truth, as he always did, but the truth reproached him.

He will not speak to the lady of his marriage.

'You do not answer,' she says.

He summons a smile. 'There are many happy arranged marriages.'

He is glad she does not ask him to name one. He tries to focus on her elaborate gold hair-covering. It is a gem-encrusted wonder with a sparkling cascade of elongated beads on either side. A challenge to recreate. A challenge he knows he can rise to.

'Do you not find –' she hesitates '– it is awkward to paint with your left hand?'

His hand halts mid-air.

'I did not mean to offend.'

He shakes his head. 'You give no offence, my lady. I was merely struck by your noticing.' For he has painted many portraits and no one has ever mentioned this singularity before. His eyes shift from her cascading gold beads to her mild face. Should he not tell this clever, observant princess what his master is really like? Why should she not know all, when he knows everything about her? As do half the English court. Even he, the artist, knows about her betrothal at eleven years to the Duke of Lorraine's young son but that they never met; that she scarcely touches alcohol; that her devout mother is loath to let her out of her sight. And more besides. Why should his master's life not also be an open book? Should he not tell her that after his fall from a horse three years ago he is almost unrecognisable? That he is well over twice her bulk, not just twice her age? That his ulcerated leg smells foul? That he is prone to rages? That the wives he should have prized he either neglected or killed?

But he is here to take a likeness only – and his generous patron is eager for the match. Among its countless benefits, an alliance with a foreign power which, like England, has rejected papal authority will help strengthen its reformed Church. The artist believes in the reformed Church. He has spent many hours taking the likenesses of scholars who speak of Scripture as muddied, its truth obscured, by man-made rules and practices. Which is why he prefers to paint Christ before theologians and pietists got to work on him. It is not that he has never painted a halo. He would just rather show Christ with a soldier sitting on his legs and another pinning down his arms, because a real person would scream and thrash if his body was nailed to a cross. When he painted Christ dead in his tomb, he modelled the Lord's body on a drowned corpse hauled from the Rhine – this time in decay. Because without real, putrid death there is no miracle of resurrection.

He does not seek to embellish truth. He only seeks to show it – clearly – so that people can accept or reject it.

As with the lady.

But herein lies the problem. She is not unbecoming, though she has this big-boned awkwardness, and he has begun to admire her. But how will such a woman, unable to converse with his master in his own language and with no musical or dancing skills, hope to please him? He is sure she cannot, whatever his patron thinks. She might even go the way of her namesake predecessor. His left hand tightens on his brush's wooden handle. For her sake, he must signal that something is amiss. A different foreign princess can then be found to take her place.

He sets to work.

****

'It is a likeness I would hang on my own wall…' The lady smiles as she gazes at the finished portrait '… if it were not destined for the King of England.'

He bows and lets out his breath. Her observational powers do not extend to noticing the changes he has made in her attire.

'I confess I am curious, though, about the changes you have made. You have not painted the pearl-studded stripe on the right of my gown – which matches the one on the left. And you have omitted the gold beads on this side –' she touches her jewelled hair-covering '– which also matched the left.'

He is suffused in heat. He cannot own that these omissions serve a purpose. That they are his signal to King Henry and Lord Cromwell that

Anna of Kleve is not all they hoped. His failure to balance ornament, in an otherwise symmetrical picture, is deliberate. As with his favouring his left hand to paint with, it delivers an impression of awkwardness – at least he hopes it does. 'A whim,' he says finally.

Her smile says his answer satisfies. But coals of fire are now heaped upon his head. Why does she not probe him more? Ask further about the man she might wed? Can he really allow her to run, unrestrained, towards a precipice? If her portrait pleases the king, and his hints go unheeded, how will she fare in England when her dangerous suitor decides he has made a mistake?

'Suppose, Master Holbein, he likes me not?'

He wants to snatch up her hand and kiss it. The courtier in him that urges the gallant falsehood '*Impossible*' is quashed for ever. Instead, he looks into her soft, brown eyes and says, 'If that were to happen, my lady, I would counsel you to go quietly.'

She looks back at him, her lips of knowledge unmoving, and gives a very slight nod. Silence ensues before she adds, 'In such an event would you visit me?'

His heartbeat quickens. 'It would be an honour, my lady.'

Slowly, her unused smile unwreathes itself.

He smiles back – in admiration.

Mongrel

Robert Carter

Once there were rabbit warrens on every rocky knoll, hidden in the tufts of paspalum and scotch thistle, punched into the walls of every dry gully, like cannonball hits. Now he had to walk half a day to find a single burrow. The second virus had been more effective than anyone imagined, killing more slowly, allowing the carrier several days to contaminate every member of the den before dropping dead.

Near the top of the hill, with a view of the entire valley, he sat down, listening to his lungs scrabbling for air. Could have jogged up that hill once, he thought, carrying a rifle and half a dozen rabbits in a bag, and not even raised a sweat. Time was a mongrel. That's what time was – a mongrel dog – the kind that waited till you turned away – when you weren't looking and then it sank its teeth into your shin bones. There was a blue cattle dog like the one from a nearby farm that always seemed to be after him – only dog he ever disliked. Just like time, he learned never to turn his back on it.

The tea from his thermos tasted like shit. 'Shouldn't put tea in a thermos,' his daughter said. 'Take a teabag.' A bloody teabag. What a stupid invention – tasteless and stale – little cardboard taggy thing went into the cup half the time. He liked the occasional tough little rolled-up tea leaf he could crunch between his teeth. Made the whole drink longer and more interesting. Not that his son and daughter-in-law would want to make anything longer and more interesting. They just wanted it over with – to get to something else that they could do quickly on their way to something else. On their way to what? But he did know. In his twenties and thirties and even into his forties he was about as relaxed and able to pause as a bullet fired from his Remington. 'You have the attention span of a traffic light', his father used to say.

Down the valley, a chickenhawk floated on the updraft, sharp against the blue, head cocked like a pistol aimed at the ground. He watched its wings barely move. Probably having as much trouble finding game as he was, he thought. He sat on an ancient sandstone boulder and noticed how the sunspots on the back of his hand matched the lichen-covered rock. It made him smile, widening his nostrils to breathe in the faint smell of eucalyptus oil from the gum leaves as the sun rounded in on them. On the upper ridges, where tractors couldn't go, a thick tree line clung to the hilltops like a Mohawk haircut. Here, for fifty thousand years, trees fell and rose, goannas and skinks hunted and magpies, crows, and galahs called each other and courted and made nests that fell with the trees.

He listened to their ancient sounds and heard something added – an unusual note. He turned his left ear towards the sound and stilled his breathing. Crying? A woman crying? It *was* a woman crying. Out here? No one came out here – he had never come across anyone this far out in the years he had been climbing the mountain. It unsettled him. Why would someone walk an hour and a half into a semi-wilderness and cry? He stood on the rock and slowly stretched upwards hoping to see where she was without being seen. He could see the top of her head, as she hunched over her knees at the bottom of a gully, a stone's throw away. He sat back down on the rock. Confused. Annoyed? It changed things – how he felt. Being alone out here was special, it was soothing, it allowed him to expand – to hear his own breath and ignore the barking of time.

Who knows why she was crying – could be some nut case – a depressed nut case? Great. What he came out here to avoid, was now following him. The crying didn't sound nutty, it didn't sound self-pitying either – it sounded more like...he wasn't quite sure...wailing? Okay, he would go over to her, see she was okay, and then get the hell away down the mountain. He took a deep breath, picked up his rifle and sack and headed towards her, making as much noise as possible to give her a chance to stop crying before he reached her. Nothing more embarrassing than being caught out in the open with nowhere to hide.

He coughed as if he had emphysema and then started whistling *'I Can See Clearly Now the Rain Has Gone...'*

As he reached the gully she looked up at him with no attempt to hide the snot and tears snailing down her cheeks.

'Are you okay?' he asked as casually as he could.

'Uh-huh,' she nodded, glancing at the rifle.

'It's only a .22,' he said dismissively. 'I'm relatively sane...and harmless.' She tried a gracious smile that failed at her eyes. He pushed on. 'Well harmless...might be a bit optimistic...never met a person who was absolutely harmless.' He watched her eyebrows rise slightly to reconsider him. He drew the thermos from the sack. 'You want some tea?'

'No...thank you.' She smiled more successfully.

Ignoring her response, he sat down in the dirt opposite, unscrewed the thermos lid which served as a mug and passed it to her.

What the hell was he doing? Was he sitting down because she was attractive? 'It tastes like shit,' he warned, hesitating to pour as she held the mug in both hands and stared at it. 'I've never seen anyone up here in the years I've been coming,' he said.

He reached into the sack and brought out a roll of toilet paper as she blew across the tea and sipped at the metal lip of the mug. 'Essential supplies,' he joked, as he tore off an arm's-length of tissue and offered it to her. She looked at him, puzzled. In her forties, he guessed, intelligent eyes, lace-up Rockports – good walking shoes. 'For your...face,' he said. She raised a hand to her face and suddenly seemed embarrassed. He turned away as she wiped and dabbed at her face. 'You want some more tea?' He noticed her hesitate, uncertain what to do with the used tissue until she tucked it away up the sleeve of her T-shirt.

‘No...thank you.’

‘Don't blame you.’

‘No...it's fine.’ She smiled as best she could, and he could see she was trying to consider his feelings.

‘I should take a jar of tea separately, but I'm too lazy,’ he said. She smiled again for his sake and stood up as he screwed the lid onto the thermos flask.

‘I'm going to go,’ she said, as she climbed carefully up the side of the gulley.‘Thank you for the tea.’

‘What about the toilet paper?’ He asked. She turned to look at him, unsure.‘I don't give toilet paper to just anyone...’ he continued. Caught off guard, she smiled genuinely.

‘*And* the toilet paper...thank you.’ She turned away and disappeared over the top of the gully. Her legs exposed under her cotton skirt as she climbed were, he noticed, white from lack of sunlight, and nice to look at. He would wait a few minutes or so before climbing after her to watch her scamper away down the mountain. It had been a long time since he had really spoken to anyone other than the mindless *good morning* and *how did you sleep* sentences that no one actually intended to have answered.

He counted to sixty and climbed out of the gully. There she was ten steps away staring back at him. Annoyingly, his face flushed.

‘I don't want to go back,’ she said.

‘Oh,’ he said, trying to recover. Did he want to know why? Uncaring husband? Ungrateful children, some failure, or loss? Did it matter? He pulled out the thermos flask. ‘It was the tea, wasn't it?’ He joked. ‘You couldn't believe anything could taste that bad...’

‘Look,’ she said, pointing behind him. He turned. In the distance the chicken hawk pulled its trigger and shot through the air, gracefully curving out of its dive at the last possible second, sailing parallel with the ground for three heartbeats before dropping into the grass and rolling over and over. He couldn't see what had been attacked, but he knew.

He could hear her running behind him, keeping pace. Downhill at speed was hard on the knees, dodging loose rocks and dead trees. ‘Yah...Yah...’ he yelled. In front of him the chicken hawk exploded upwards, its beautiful wings unfolding, climbing invisible stairs. He turned and motioned for her to move quietly, as he searched the surrounding area. There it was under a wild blackberry bush. He slowly moved closer, aware of her two steps behind him. He pointed to the blackberry bush. The rabbit, no more than six weeks old he estimated, instinctively sat as still as it could, shivering and terrified. The hawk had done what he knew it would. He raised the rifle and sighted carefully. Behind him, he heard her shout as he pulled the trigger.

‘No!’

Kneeling down, he reached into the blackberry bush, spiking and tearing the soft skin of his inside wrist as he pulled the rabbit out by its back legs. He turned and held it up for her to see. She closed her eyes and turned away angrily.

'The hawk tore its eyes,' he said.

'Oh God...' she turned to look at him, her hand covering her mouth.

'It can't hold the weight of the rabbit for long... It needs to disable it and that's the quickest way.'

'What will you do with it?' she asked, still turned away from him.

'Leave him for the hawk now he can't feel anything.'

Walking back to the gully, she kept alongside him, glancing back every few steps.

'You didn't ask why I was crying,' she said.

'If you wanted to tell someone, you wouldn't have come out here.' He knew she was looking at him, summing him up.

'I'm sorry I shouted at you...about the rabbit.'

'You want some more tea?' he asked, as they reached the gully.

Looking out across the foothills, as he passed the mug to her, he could see clouds hunching and bruising as they ballooned towards them. 'Storm,' he said, tilting his forehead to the west. She twisted to look.

'Great...caps off my perfect day.'

'Not yours to cap off,' he said. He watched her puzzle and then soften.

'Good point.'

'There's not much cover up here...from the rain,' he said.

'It's only water.'

'Good point.' He smiled, already liking her.

'My husband says I'm too sensitive.' She passed the mug back to him.

'Too sensitive?'

'Yes.'

'I thought sensitive was good.'

'I have unrealistic expectations...'

'Of what?'

'Everything.'

'Everything, huh? Well, at least you're consistent.'

She smiled and shook her head. 'What about you...you sit out here waiting for injured rabbits?'

'No, mostly I shoot the ones staggering around with blood running out of their ears from the virus.'

'Oh, God...'

'My father taught me at eight years of age to shoot, skin, gut...and crack their necks if necessary with my bare hands.' He held out his hands with his fingers splayed and saw again the sun damage. Was he trying to shock her? Impress her? 'But only if we were going to eat them.'

'Not for sport'

'No.'

'But you don't do that anymore?'

'No, I don't.'

She looked at the sack. 'What's that for?'

'I take the infected ones home and bury them... Their mates will come sniffing for them.'

'And catch the virus?'

He nods and watches her head move in time with his. 'We should go...storm's moving quickly.'

She doesn't answer or move to go. He looks past her for the chicken hawk, wondering whether it will come back for the dead rabbit. Rising around him, he could smell what he read once, were earth-type pheromones, released by the hot ground attempting to seduce rain. Waiting. Dry land, always waiting. When her face turned away down towards the flat paddocks, he looked at her closely and wondered what it would be like to stretch her arms back against the hot grass and have sex with her – rut like rabbits. He felt the rush of blood and excitement and it made him smile. It had been a long time. She was married. And crying. It was going to rain. He shook his head.

'I've interrupted your...your solitude...haven't I?' she said quietly.

He grinned at her. 'Yes, you have.'

'Shall we walk down together?'

He headed for the rusted bones of an old Massey Ferguson tractor on the flats near the creek. Over the years he had watched it slowly take on the red-brown colour of the exposed soil, its tyres and attached parts having been raided by local farmers as their needs arose. She walked alongside him, and he was aware how their shoulders bumped at various times, hers thin and bony through her cotton T-shirt. He allowed himself to brush up against her by accident at every ditch and fallen log. They approached the blackberry bush and he noticed that she looked at the dead rabbit deliberately as they passed.

'Will the hawk come back to it?'

'Probably not,' he said. 'Maybe after we're gone.'

'Look,' she said, pointing to the west. 'You can see the rain coming towards us across those hills.'

'Uh-huh... Not gonna outrun it.'

'Shall we try?' She asked.

It made him smile. He grabbed her hand and took off, ignoring her squeals. Down the face of the hill he ran, tilting his body forward, risking a fall, but anchored by her weight. Between breaths, he heard her laughter racing ahead of them. As they neared the tractor, the rain struck. Large wind-whipped drops that stained the dry, rusted metal and split in wet veins down the curve of the mudguards. He stopped running, let go of her hand, breathing hard and lifted the sack over their heads for shelter.

‘Don't bother,’ she laughed. ‘We’re drenched...doomed.’

He watched her climb up onto the tractor and sit where the seat once attached. He lowered the sack and pulled it over his rifle, barrel first.

She was pointing past him – behind him – standing up on the tractor footplates, her eyes wide. He turned and stopped the dog dead. Mongrel blue cattle dog. About to attack before he turned – easing its body closer to the ground, wagging its tail deceptively.

‘Bastard,’ he accused it. The dog thumped its tail up and down twice and waited in the wet grass, its eyes dark and patient. ‘I could shoot you…always could have,’ he said. ‘And buried you out here…’

‘Get up here,’ she called through the rain. He glanced at her and back at the dog to see that even in the two seconds he had turned away, the dog had crept a half step closer.

‘He won't bite while I'm watching,’ he answered her over his shoulder. From the sack, he withdrew the rifle smoothly, clicked off the safety, and levelled it at the dog's head.

‘What are you doing?’ She shouted at him.

‘The bastard’s always there...always after me,’ he yelled back to her.

‘You can't kill it!’

He saw the concern on her face, the rain drizzling into her open mouth, the soaked clothes showing her body, the silliness and beauty of her mounted on the decaying tractor in the rain. He was old – the word he hated – most of his life was over, and he didn't want any part of it to be over. He sighted between the dog's eyes, blinking away the rain that lodged between his eyelashes and dripped in a watery curtain blurring everything...everything. Yet here he was in his favourite place in the world with a beautiful, laughing, crying woman in the rain, and the creeping dog had not yet managed to bite him – not yet.

‘Bang!’ he said to the dog, who lifted and swept his tail from side to side as steady as a metronome.

Onassis and Hoxha

Juliet Hill

The narrow stretch of the sea had always held on to its secrets but sometimes abandoned objects would wash up on the beach at Saranda. Tomor would look out at the Corfu channel, wondering if these treasures had come from a yacht like the one belonging to Aristotle Onassis: a French perfume bottle, a ripped silk scarf, even a Duke Ellington record. It was too worn away by the sea to play on his parents' ancient player but he kept it in a box under the bed and took it out from time to time.

Tomor's father said Onassis was irresistible to women and would take them on his luxury yacht to sail around the Mediterranean. His father gleaned the information from forbidden magazines or Italian radio broadcasts which crackled through on a tiny receiver when they were sure of complete solitude. He also claimed to have seen the yacht sail past, complete with Maria Callas on deck, but Tomor found that hard to believe. He could visualise fascinated Albanians reaching for hidden binoculars and focusing on the vessel, trying to get a glimpse of the mosaic dance floor which could be lowered to make an instant swimming-pool or the huge spiral staircase that dominated the central part of the boat, but he never heard of a single sighting beyond his father's imaginary one.

When Tomor's father found out about Onassis's death he intoned that it was the end of an era. Tomor didn't believe that either. His father had said the same thing two years earlier, hope and emotion creeping into his dry voice, when President Hoxha suffered a devastating heart attack. Nothing changed. Unlike Onassis, Hoxha seemed to be invincible.

Looking out of his window forty years later with the Straits directly ahead, and the island of Corfu so close, it was hard to believe that these waters had once only been the preserve of a few Greek fishermen, clinging to the Corfu coast to avoid coming anywhere near the heavily mined Albanian side. Now the water swarmed with assorted yachts, fishing boats and ferries and he reflected that it would probably be more dangerous to swim across than it had been then. He could see the coast of Corfu as clear as ever, its tiny inlets, harbours and cottages contrasting with the luxury houses clinging to the edge of low cliffs.

Visitors came regularly from Corfu, skimming over the water and bumping along pot-holed roads to the nearby Roman ruins of Butrint. A few more intrepid backpackers chose to stay in Saranda's hotels and guest houses, convinced that they'd found the next hot spot. It was somewhere new for their gap year, or whatever they called it, giving them a one-upmanship over their friends who'd gone to Vietnam or Bolivia.

Tomor heard somebody enter the room and turned to see his wife, Adelina, carefully folding empty plastic bags and putting them in her handbag.

'You don't have to do that. They'll give you more at the supermarket.'

'I know.'

Old habits.

After Adelina had gone he looked out of the window again. The beach was still empty, the backpackers sleeping off their hangovers, and it was still possible to remember how quiet it had been in the old days. The nights were different. Now there were kids on the beach till the early hours, shouting and playing loud music while young local men on mopeds roared up and down the esplanade, unaware or ignorant of the price that had been paid by earlier generations. The lights were never dimmed and the neon pushed its way into his house, however much he tried to block it out.

Before, the nights were completely silent and light came only from the stars. Few wanted to risk being questioned about why they were out, and people huddled in the comparative safety of their grey concrete homes, listening to the news on the national radio station. They would filter and interpret the information as best they could, in an attempt to make sense of their own lives, trying to mentally compensate for the shrieking absence of things that they knew were happening but were never mentioned.

It was on a night like that when Tomor and Ilir set out. They'd been planning it for a few months and felt finally ready. They'd trained every day until exhaustion set in, trying to build their strength for something that they couldn't predict. How could they know what dangers there'd be? They'd heard tales of people who'd made it, young men their age who'd swum the channel and built a new life in Corfu but of course nobody could verify these stories and very few people even wanted to talk about the subject.

'Have some more stew. You'll need it.'

Tomor's mother somehow knew something was up, the way of mothers everywhere, though she said nothing. When he'd first met Ilir at primary school she'd concealed her misgivings about their friendship, trying not to let her own worries infect his life and calmly answering his questions about the Greek minority in Saranda. His father, despite his admiration for Onassis could only mutter, *count your fingers,* after shaking hands with a Greek.

But as an adult Tomor realised just how worried they'd been about the possible effects on his family of his closeness with Ilir. Now he and his mother acknowledged in silence that the less she knew about their plans the better.

'I'm fine Mum. I promised Ilir I'd go over to help him fix his radio.'

'Your father will be back soon. Don't you want to stay and say hello?'

'I'll see him later.'

He'd already said a final goodbye to his father early that morning, though his father hadn't known it. He wanted to tell him that if it hadn't been for his tales of Onassis and luxury yachts, of all-night balls and glamorous foreign guests, Tomor mightn't have felt this urge to go. Most of his other friends didn't feel that need. They talked about escaping to the west but for them, it was an abstract idea, a promised land where they would be millionaires and have access to unlimited beautiful women and luxury food. But given the choice, they'd have gone for a high party position, a meaner, shabbier reward.

Tomor's interest in the world beyond Saranda was nourished by Ilir's family. Ilir's grandparents would talk of the old days, their old days. His mother would try to stop them but they were beyond telling, and Tomor would listen to their tales of Greek life, marvelling as they switched between Albanian and Greek to emphasise a particular point or when something was untranslatable. They spoke of small villages where life revolved around the church, and religious festivals dominated the calendar; they spoke of whitewashed houses and unlimited fish in the sea, of small bakeries and bars, of dances and parties. Sometimes they cried as they remembered family and friends on the other side of the endless electrified fence that separated the two countries, but when this happened they switched to Greek and Tomor would quickly lose the thread.

He once asked Ilir why his parents never spoke Greek.

'They do. But not when other people are around. My father says it's better not to draw attention to ourselves.'

'But you don't speak it.'

Ilir laughed. He had the kind of chuckling laugh that always made Tomor want to join in and he found himself smiling.

'You've just never heard me.'

It might have been that moment that Tomor thought: *if I do the swim I should go with Ilir so that one of us can communicate when we arrive*. Or it might have been that he'd already decided to ask him to come and that just confirmed that it was the right decision. Whatever it was, he mentioned it to him that night.

Ilir didn't laugh this time.

'Swim across the sea? Are you mad? There are mines, searchlights, you've seen them. We'd get picked up in no time. They'd probably shoot us on sight.'

'Not if we time it well. It's been done before.'

'You don't know that for sure.'

'Old mother Vrioni's son never came back.'

'He could be in a prison camp. She's not going to say, is she? And anyway, even if we weren't shot, do you really think we could swim that far? God knows, it's at least ten kilometres from here and there's no way we could get down the coast to start somewhere closer.'

But Tomor had planted the seed and soon Ilir and he were talking about it more seriously, taking long walks to discuss their plans in depth. In this, they followed the example of their elders. Nobody talked about serious subjects unless they were outside and alone, and even then they constantly looked around and dropped their voices in a kind of unconscious reflex action. There had always been rumours about President Hoxha's secret scientific experiments and when paranoia set in, as it frequently did, it didn't seem absurd that he could have developed some mind-reading tool or even a listening device implanted in peoples bodies or animals. After all, the secret police always seemed to know everything.

Sometimes they allowed themselves to dream. Tomor would tell Ilir the stories about Onassis and his famous friends, and they'd plan how they'd build a luxury yacht and sail it around all of the Mediterranean. Ilir's dream was more modest.

'My father says that the fascists are no longer in charge in Greece. If I can make a life there, maybe I can get my parents out and we can set up a business; just the family, the way my grandparents talk about it.'

Soon their swim became an accepted fact and by the 1980s when the regime finally lost its last deep-pocketed ally, Tomor decided that the time was right.

And now he was leaving for Ilir's house where they would wait a few more hours before making their way to the quietest stretch of coast they could get to without leaving the town boundaries. Tomor's mother called him back.

'Take this.'

She was holding a silver metal cross on a chain. He'd never seen one close up before and he certainly had no idea that his mother had her own treasure secreted away, just as he had his Duke Ellington record hidden in the box under the bed.

'What's that?'

'I want you to wear it. For safety.'

He wouldn't be safe for five minutes with something like that hanging around his neck, but he knew what she meant. He put it on carefully and pushed it down underneath his jersey and shirt so that there wasn't even an outline showing. Then he kissed his mother, picked up his small duffel bag and left.

They waited until after midnight before leaving Ilir's house and by then there was nothing on the roads, not even a military patrol. The moon was nearly full, lighting their pale faces and giving them an unexpectedly starring role in the dark of the night. The stars were clear on the Albanian side but looking across the water Tomor was able to see the much brighter lights of Corfu dazzling across the water and shaming his silent town. Perhaps even now the people of Corfu were celebrating some local festival, laughing, drinking and dancing, while their more subdued neighbours across the channel were in bed early, following a deep-rooted instinct to avoid anything that might draw attention.

The two of them made their way slowly south on the Kasamil road, ready to jump to one side and hide behind the scrubby bushes at any moment. It was a warm night with a light breeze coming in from the sea, and as he breathed in the salty night air, Tomor realised that he'd never been out this late before, not even on New Year's Eve. He couldn't imagine a life in which you went out at night for pleasure.

The rocky promontory they'd chosen after weeks of intense deliberation was as far from the beach as they dared go, and had the advantage that they could climb down and shelter among the boulders while timing the sweeps of the searchlights and waiting for the right moment.

'What was that?'

They were near the point where they were planning to descend to the rocks when they heard it. The rough diesel cough of a military truck, a vehicle they both learnt to distinguish from a young age. It had to be a patrol; nobody else would be out at this time unless they were on official business. Tomor looked around desperately, trying to find something, anything that they could use for shelter.

'Over here!'

Ilir pushed him ahead and they ran across some scrubland and hid in a group of anaemic-looking trees near the edge of the cliff. They heard the truck stop for a while and deep voices muttering inaudible comments as soldiers flashed torchlights briefly around the immediate area, but then it left, leaving an aroma of exhaust fumes and cigarette smoke in the warm night air. Tomor and Ilir waited for what felt like at least an hour before beginning to venture out from their hiding place, not believing their luck and flinching at every sound. Ilir crawled towards the edge of the cliff and began to make his way down to the rocks but Tomor hung back, hissing in his direction.

'What if they come back? They're not stupid. Let's wait a bit longer.'

And then he saw it. A solid beam of light making its way across the grass. There was no sound just the moving torchlight and he knew that he couldn't move or draw attention to himself, so he stood, trembling, like a lizard frozen on a wall. There was another light and then another. An army of torches marching across the scrubby grass, the lights bobbing up and down with the soldiers' strides and now with the sound of muttered orders and muted replies.

When he ran through the scene in his mind later, his one regret was turning his head a fraction to check for Ilir. He should have remained still, pretending he was alone, but it was too late. Two of the torches were suddenly focused directly on him and he knew there was no way out.

He couldn't regret his second involuntary movement although it haunted him for a long time afterwards. What else would he have done? It was as natural as remembering his mother's face. His hand, which had been still by his side suddenly reached towards his chest and felt for the cross under his clothes, almost as if he believed all that stuff and was trying to tap into the power of the symbol. He wanted to feel it there, not just for his mother but because it was something that they – the authorities, the soldiers, the police – couldn't control.

'Strip him.'

It was the commanding officer. Tomor couldn't see him through the torchlight but his voice came from above. As they pushed him over and ripped off his clothes, kicking him around like a football, he recognised one of them as the tall soldier he'd seen in the square earlier that day, sitting smoking a cigarette and looking out to sea. Tomor had caught his eye as he passed and felt the soldier's gaze on his back as he walked away towards the bakery. It didn't seem impossible that the soldier had sensed his guilt and figured out his plans.

They threw him in the back of a truck and began the bumpy journey to the police station. The cross had been ripped from his neck and he didn't see it again until much later when it reappeared in the hands of his torturers and was pressed into service in ways he'd spent a long time trying to forget.

When he returned home, nobody spoke of Ilir. The family had left or been forced out, and when Tomor asked after them, people shook their heads and hurried away. It was as if they'd never been there. In his own house, his father had died and his mother rarely spoke. She cried for a full day when he hobbled through the front door a year after his arrest, but then retreated into her silence, and he felt guilty even asking her simple questions. She never mentioned the cross and neither did he.

He thought a lot about Ilir during the years when nobody seemed to be in charge of the country and a kind of low level anarchy bubbled under the surface. He liked to imagine his friend sipping cocktails on the deck of a yacht with Duke Ellington playing in the background, Onassis-style, or sitting in a brightly-painted Corfu restaurant watching the sun go down with a brandy and a cigarette. But at night Hoxha and his henchmen still reigned. At night Ilir was caught by searchlights and machine-gunned in the water or blown up by a mine and left in bloody pieces to get caught in the seaweed or pecked at by hungry fishes. What was left of his face would stare with an expression of angry disappointment and Tomor would jerk awake with a concrete block of guilt pressing hard against his chest. One unwanted reflex had betrayed his friend, the other his mother's mysterious beliefs. But the weight was beginning to diminish and Tomor could breathe a little easier every year. He'd never forget Ilir and his chuckling laugh, but he had to leave him there, in the water.

He heard Adelina come in and start to unpack the shopping. She was singing to herself. He took one last look at the stretch of sea which had dictated the course of his life and went downstairs to help her.

Selfish Kisses and Early Polaroids

James Woolf

Navigating his way cautiously through the hedge tunnel, he emerges into aching brightness. For the first time in months, he feels a quiver of pleasure, as if a ray of sunshine were ricocheting inside him.

The garden is perfect. At once rambunctious and guardedly formal – it is a truly English combination. A sundial on the path before him leads to an arbour shaded bench; he will need shade today. With lightness in his gait, the celebrated filmmaker begins to explore, noting the bellflowers and mountain mist pinks overhanging the path.

His curiosity had been piqued by a letter explaining that the garden was a gift from the 18th century philanthropist Ralph Allen to a lady with whom he'd been romantically entwined.

He sits on the bench and sighs with satisfaction. There are no traffic sounds, just the gentle whisper of leaves and intermittent bird calls. It had been a condition of his visit that the talks should happen outside London, and that he should be supplied with a quiet outdoor location where he will not be disturbed. Looking around him he can see several similar paths each leading to a bench. There is a stone wall, crumbling deliciously, and just the right scattering of sculptures, resolute and weather-beaten, and two large urns displaying more flowers.

Movement. A head in a hat turns towards him. He is not alone. The head is in a far corner of the garden, and therefore indistinct. But it is there nevertheless. And it should not be!

Those of you who have read and understood Stephen Hawking's *A Brief History of Time* will be aware that time and space are intimately linked, and that space-time can become warped, perhaps creating wormholes. Warping of time is insignificant on this planet, in comparison to, say, in a black hole, which makes it difficult to comprehend which scientific laws have permitted this occurrence.

The young lady, for it is a young lady, also seems surprised that she has company, and makes her way purposefully towards the film maker. She is dressed in what must be the English fashion: a pale cotton ground-length dress, Spencer jacket, and wide-brimmed straw-hat, presumably on account of the sun.

'Your name, sir, and what you are doing here?'

His English, although passable, is not perfect. It takes a moment for him to register the question.

'I must tell you,' he says, 'that this garden was a promise by Sebastian Taylor. It is for my use only. I am asking you to leave so that I can be here alone.'

'You are mistaken, sir. I have the sole use of this garden, belonging as it does to my dear friend Eliza Calvert. She is in Oxford and expressly permitted me to visit whenever I wish.'

'I have not heard of this Eliza Calvert!'

'Nor I of Sebastian Taylor!'

They have reached an impasse, the point at which it would be unwise to voice further thoughts. She would like to say that he has clearly taken leave of his senses. He would like to tell her to go to hell. They remain silent for a minute more instead.

'Clearly, we cannot both be right,' she ventures. He agrees with this.

As neither is willing to relinquish the space, they explore how they might share it, 'just for this afternoon of course'. A quick tour of the garden establishes that there are five benches. Providing they choose who sits on which with care, they can surely manage well enough without disturbing each other.

The plan proves flawed. He can see her from the corner of his eye, moving fractionally each time she turns the page of her book. Closing his eyes does not assist. Just the thought that she is there disturbs his tranquillity. He rises from his seat and suggests that they try sitting on two completely different benches but, soon afterwards, she returns in a state of agitation.

'It is no good! I keep noticing your legs fidgeting, Mr...? I still do not know your name.'

'Ingmar Bergman.' His eyes narrow, waiting for her reaction.

'And I am Jane,' she says, sitting next to him. 'We may as well share this bench as we are clearly too selfish to occupy one each.'

He cannot help smiling. This inconsequential looking woman at least has the advantage of being quick-witted.

'You will know my work,' he continues. '*The Seventh Seal, Wild Strawberries, Through a Glass Darkly...*'

'You can stop, Mr Bergman. I do not know any of them. I too am a writer, although not yet published.'

'And your name again?'

'Jane Austen.'

The filmmaker's face reddens and his eyes widen so much that she fears he has been taken ill.

'This is most significant,' he says.

He has arisen in some confusion.

'I must leave, however. I have a meeting, but this moment...it will stay with me. You will be published, Miss Austen. I have a biography... But I must leave.'

He is gone even before she utters a puzzled goodbye.

We too will never understand how this moment happened or how it is to be repeated the following day. As Stephen Hawking remarked, 'No government agency can be seen spending public money on anything as way out as time travel.' Although theoretically, he admitted, you could travel from one side of the galaxy to the other in a week through a wormhole, then journey back through another and arrive home before you set out.

He is already seated on his bench the next morning. She joins him without hesitation.

'You mentioned that I am to be published, Mr Bergman...?'

'Yes, several books. You will be a household name.'

Her wide forehead flushes and a muscle twitches near her eye.

'But what books are these?'

'I don't know their names, damn it – something, I think...about prejudice? Or pride? Or both. I watched this terrible adaptation...'

She's now convinced, as he wriggles – as if in pain – struggling to recall details of books she has never written, that he suffers from lunacy, a diagnosis confirmed by his saying that the year is 1976 and he was recently arrested for tax fraud.

'Tax fraud?'

'I've got it,' he shrieks. 'The infuriating Mr Darcy! And Miss...Miss Bennet!'

'*First Impressions*? My father tried sending it to a publisher, but I've long since abandoned that novel...'

'Then you must not!'

'I have not written for two years. I am unable. Ever since we came to Bath.'

'And I cannot make films in Sweden. Not while I'm under investigation. It appears we are together in this crisis.'

'But you said I am to be a celebrated author?'

'Of course, yes. I have your biography sitting on my shelf. Unread, I must admit. It had its translation into Swedish by a close friend. He has been exasperating me, trying to discuss it.'

'Unread, did you say?'

'Unopened, actually. I knew your face. The cover drawing has an excellent likeness.'

There is so much information to assimilate. Worldwide fame lasting more than a century! Darcy and Elizabeth appearing in a different book – *Prejudice and Pride*, not a bad title... But some hurt feelings to brush aside too. That he has a biography of her, translated by his friend. And he has not cared enough about him, or it, or her, to have opened it...

'How utterly selfish you are!'

Her remark produces a profound effect. He rises with a look of alarm, walks in a pained shuffle, runs his hand along a hedge and sits heavily back down.

'It is the only way that artists can be. The act of creation is selfish. And conceited. First you must feel you have something to say. And then you must slam doors to so many sides of your life. A magnificent artist is a despicable person! He has no time for anyone, or anything. Except for himself and his damn projects.'

'So you have never been married, Mr Bergman?'

'Ha! I am on number five!'

'Five? That is rather a lot.'

'I am now – what do you say? – in my stride. And you?'

A purple butterfly zig-zags in front of her. They watch as it rises and disappears.

'Nothing,' she says bleakly. 'I was engaged, for one evening only. I spent the night picturing myself slipping into matrimonial obscurity and broke it off the very next day.'

'A sensible decision! The world has enjoyed your books far more than it would have done your children!'

They laugh and it seems that they might be friends after all. Timeless places can perhaps connect people from different times.

'You know Mr Bergman, we must never speak a word about our meetings. We really must not.'

'Of course. We would both be considered totally insane. It would be very dangerous to our reputations.'

'We have met though for a reason, I'm sure.'

The next day, he carries a small cardboard box which she surveys with interest. It is something he says that he has desired for several years and only now has he bought one in a chemist in Bath.

'What are you doing in Bath, Mr Bergman? I'm sorry I haven't asked before, I've been very remiss.'

'I have been talking to a British company about making a film in English. The plan was for it also to be shot here. Unfortunately, the discussions have amounted to nothing. I return to Sweden tomorrow.'

Noticing that he is carefully monitoring her reaction, she remarks, as cheerfully as she can muster, that it will be wonderful for him to be back home. His wife and family must be missing him so much. They'll be delighted that he has returned early.

Her reaction disappoints him. So he explains why he must not make the film. The British producers were pompous, interfering and brimming with silly ideas. He could not allow them to be blundering in front of his film. It would have been impossible!

'I do not understand *films*, Mr Bergman. I do not know what you are saying.'

'You must come back to Sweden with me,' he says suddenly. 'You know what it is to be an artist. And you are unimpressed by my achievements. I like that. You will be my perfect partner!'

'It cannot be. You are already married.'

'Yes, and so you keep reminding me!'

'You must find me very restrained.'

'Can't you see? I've wasted my life trying to capture actors' souls on celluloid.'

'I do not understand *celluloid*. I detest even the sound of the word.'

'I'm an utterly selfish person. You said so yourself.'

'Come come! Selfishness we must forgive. After all, there's no hope of a cure.'

'Yes, and you should put that in one of your very English books too!'

She is silent.

'I am sorry, Miss Austen. I am probably not good at saying goodbye.'

He opens the box.

'This is my Polaroid. Yes, you can touch it.'

Then, pulling her by the hand, he sweeps her across the garden towards a statue of Eros. Positioning the camera on a sundial, he fiddles with the buttons before rushing back.

Seconds later, the shiny card drops into her hand and they stare as the colours form. There they are! Captured together, either side of the *God of Love*, smiling coyly.

'My films have images like this. But the people – they move and speak. That's how I tell my stories!'

'And you must continue.' Her eyes swell with tears.

'And you must keep the photograph. I have the biography, remember? I will read it as soon as I am home. I believe everything will turn out very well for you.'

Placing one hand on Eros's head, she looks the filmmaker in the eye and plants a kiss firmly on his lips.

'There, you see!' she says. 'Entirely selfish.'

'It must be forgiven,' he responds gravely.

Silver Bird

David Shelley Jones

He never should have agreed to an interview. Mr Tamamoto is becoming more certain of this as each day passes and now it is too late. By his reckoning, the young American woman is already in the air, reclining in her seat, having a drink, not thinking too much about the job at hand. He tries to remember her name. Was it Liz, or Lola or Libby? – definitely something beginning with an *l* . He knows there must be others with her. He imagines them all having a little party on their way to Japan. Americans in the sky! Just like before.

The last time Tamamoto took a long flight was years ago when he returned from the United States. He had spent a few years in San Francisco after the war as a marketing manager for an electronics company. His English was good back then. Now it's rusty and he's made them well aware of the fact. He's been reassured that they will come with a translator – but how can he tell if he is being interpreted correctly? He's known Japanese translators to make a hash of things and the subject is just so sensitive, *too* sensitive, which is why he should have politely declined the request.

'What do you want me to do, lost souls?' He asks the question under his breath, with his eyes closed, as he drifts amongst the long-ago faces – the shopkeepers, the soldiers, the children, the scurrying civilians. He goes on muttering until the voice of his grandson draws him back to the present.

'Why do you bathe every evening in the thermal springs, Grandpa?'

He knows he has been talking to himself again and he is impressed at such a tactful approach from someone so young. He puts down his newspaper and holds the boy in his steady, old man's gaze.

'I go there to dream.'

Tamamoto has six grandchildren and this boy is his favourite. *The boy is so astute*, he thinks, *so direct*. They are alone together in a small room of mixed Japanese and Western-style while the others are out shopping. Tamamoto has given up the tradition of low seating in the interest of comfort. He sits in a large armchair with the boy at his feet on a tatami mat. The TV is on, but neither is watching.

'Do you want to know what I dreamt about yesterday, Sato?'

'Yes, Grandpa, tell me.' The boy looks up at him. He isn't sure if the child is just being polite, but he is glad to continue.

'I dreamt of flowers, the flowers that grew the year after the war. You should have seen them, Sato, morning glory and daylilies, sickle senna and purslane, goosefoot and feverfew, bluets and clotbur. Such an abundance amidst the ruins. You wouldn't have believed it.'

He feels obliged to explain the many benefits of a hot bath and how, long ago, ancient hands had tamed the springs, channelled the steaming rivulets down village streets so that life would take hold and bloom in the alpine wilderness.

He would like to continue, but he can see that the boy is losing interest and he regrets his habit of lapsing into a monologue. He stops talking and silence returns. Sato resumes teasing the cat and he tries to refocus on his newspaper. He enjoys the silence. It is a break from the onslaught of words. He is sick of words. The world is full of too much talking and not enough thinking; although he is about to add quite a few more words to the ether himself when the Americans come. He always said he'd never give an interview, but what could he say? The money was just too good: a huge donation to the local hospital. There wasn't much choice when he thinks about it.

Before long, his mind puts out to sea once more. His daydreaming is getting worse. Lately, he has found himself exploring the hazy coastline of childhood memory, sailing further into all its bays and estuaries, coming up close to the shore, so that the details, at last, returned to focus.

The brief wail of an air raid siren is followed by the impatient voice of his mother.

'Why does everything take so long with you, Hiraku? Pay attention! Hurry up!'

He remembers his mother's painful grip as she pulls him by the arm towards the shelter. He is a child again, about the age of his grandson. He is tired of all the air raid drills. Strangely, his mother's appearance does not seem at all in keeping with the family photographs that he now keeps in a shoebox beneath his bed. She is gaunt and unsmiling. Her hair is loose. It is not done up in the elaborate, traditional style of the photographs. Then his mother's face vanishes and he is standing at the front of their old house with his parents on either side. He cannot see them, but he knows they are there, he can sense their presence. An uncle, a famous army commander, is coming to tea. There has been a flurry of activity and now they are waiting outside in the rain, holding umbrellas, staring down the road.

Tamamoto wakes up with a start to find himself back in the living room. He has a cramp and massages his leg as he looks about, re-orientating himself. The TV is still on in the corner with the volume turned down. Sato is gone. *Typical*, he thinks, *the boy can't keep still for two minutes. What's the matter with young people these days?*

After several minutes his leg is better. He stops the massaging and listens for sounds of household activity, his hearing being the only faculty that is still in top form, which is remarkable given his history. He detects no signs of life and is a little put out. Although enjoying the peace and quiet, he needs his family. He feels lucky to have them around. His fugues are becoming more real and he worries that he is gradually losing his mind. Until recently, travels within the confines of his skull have been dreams; but lately, they have been assuming an increasingly vivid reality. He is beginning to feel that he can reach out and touch the flowers of years ago, smell the acrid smoke, hear the rustle of the skirts of pretty girls. He's seen it happen, the mental slippage that starts slowly and then accelerates like a retaining wall collapsing. There's Shigeyoshi, for example, down the road, on his own, once sharp as a knife, now *puttsun*, mad as a March hare. Hiraku is starting to conclude that the only thing between him and madness is his family. They are his mooring lines. That's how it seems as his chin sinks into his chest and he falls asleep again...

'Not long, not long now.' Was it his father's or his mother's voice?

A long, black Toyota staff car appears and parks outside the gate. It is the most magnificent car he has ever seen. His uncle is sitting in the back. A young corporal is at the wheel. As soon as the car comes to a halt, the young corporal springs out of his seat to open the door for his uncle and then stands to attention in the rain until they go inside.

His uncle takes the place of honour, kneeling at the far end of their small reception room, while the floral figure of his mother leans over a charcoal burner. His uncle is wearing a beautiful uniform, starched and green, with the large cuff insignias of a senior officer. He is also wearing a *senninbari*, a red sash belt made of a thousand stitches. The belt is meant to ward off bullets. The belt and the confident manner of his uncle, the easy laugh and broad gestures, make him feel that, in the end, everything will be all right. Of course, it isn't all right. His uncle will die in Okinawa just six weeks from now.

And so it goes. The vivid recollections march past like an endless column of soldiers, no matter how hard he tries to hold on to the present.

Tamamoto would usually take the waters after dinner because his favourite onsen is usually empty at this time. He would walk down to the steaming bathhouse in nothing but an old, frayed kimono even when it is blizzarding and the streets are deserted. There is nothing like the peace of a quiet onsen. Body and mind can find release. The present can be set adrift. Time does not matter. Everything is reduced: to minerals, to elements, to heat. Whole epochs hang suspended in the vapours.

'I go there to forget.'

This is the answer Tamamoto would like to have given Sato. He can dream, though. With dreams, it is possible to fuse the memories of childhood with the seventy years that followed. With dreams, everything can be reconciled.

As soon as the others return and he is relieved from babysitting, he changes and leaves for the bathhouse. It is beautiful outside. The first snow of the season is drifting down upon the cedar groves, upon the wooden eaves and cobbled streets, upon the locals stooping forward against the flurries. He had known it would snow. He could sense it coming from the flight of sparrows, the colour of the sky, the pattern of falling leaves.

Tamamoto is pleased to find the onsen empty as anticipated. He hangs his kimono on a hook in the small wooden anteroom and showers before slowly lowering himself into the shallow, steaming pool. He stretches out until the water reaches his neck and he can rest his head on the cold granite rim.

He closes his eyes and listens to the gurgle of the crusted tap playing perfect counterpoint to the silence of falling snow. Despite the peace, he is conscious of the jets of boiling water far below; how they press ferociously upwards through the fracture lines of rock only to end the journey in gentle, steaming pools, like screams attenuated to whispers.

This is how his dreams begin – with heat and cold, lightness and darkness, pressure and release. Then his thoughts can wander. The running tap grows silent and in the silence the silver bird returns.

Tamamoto's fugues are many but the silver bird is usually the opening bar – the first note a speck of glinting fuselage in the bright, early morning sun. Then the plane. High up in a clear blue sky...

The war had taken the family to the Chugoku region where his father worked as an engineer. Every morning at precisely 8 a.m., to demonstrate air superiority, an American reconnaissance plane flew across the southern sky. Hiraku Tamamoto looked for it as he walked to school. He called the aircraft *The Silver Bird*. It was a marvellous sight, that lonely plane in the springtime month of May when the cherry blossoms were in bloom. It was a distant blinking mirror, a morning star! How high it flew! There was not a sound.

Then August came. The flowers disappeared. The silver bird flew in wider arcs. The streets grew silent. The children stopped playing games. He often had to hold a place in the snaking lines of people waiting to be given food.

'Please play with me, Papa,' he would implore.

'When Japan wins. When we win.' This was always the reply but the words sounded hollow even to the ears of a child. There was no longer any time for daydreaming, no time for observing the small details of nature that held him in thrall. He had to join the after-school work parties. There was endless digging, fetching, carrying.

The cat died the day before he ran away. It had grown thin. Tufts of fur came out in handfuls. When it vomited on the floor, his father killed it with a shovel in the backyard next to the apple tree. Young Tamamoto wasn't meant to see but he had come home from school early.

The next morning, before anyone was awake, he ran away. He found rice and pickled vegetables and wrapped them in greased paper before placing them in the pannier of his bicycle together with a flask of water. He set off, taking care with the front door and the creaking gate. He pedalled furiously until town gave way to country and his thin legs settled into a steady, even rhythm. A light breeze rippled through the trees. The birds were singing. He would reach Hiroshima by daybreak.

Tamamoto grows dizzy from the steam and heat and steps out of the hot water. He has learned to do this carefully, as he fainted once and cut his head and he had to be stitched up by the local doctor.

After showering, he looks at himself in the mirror. He has grown used to the burden of deformity, his purple twisted arm, the railway junction of keloid scars on his abdomen, his short right leg with the foot turned inwards. He is a *hibakusha*, an affected person, although he counts himself lucky that he has not acquired leukaemia or cataracts or any other long-term effects of radiation. An ageing body is just another outrage.

He closes the ancient wooden door behind him and looks about for Sato and his bicycle. The boy often rides down to meet him and see him home. He knows that this is under the direction of his daughter, but he is touched all the same. And sure enough, there is Sato across the road, standing under the streetlamp while snowflakes gather on his hood and jacket. The boy is absorbed in freeing a pocket zipper and hasn't noticed his grandfather come out. Although it is extremely cold, Tamamoto pauses for a moment to watch the boy's intense concentration, his oblivion to everything except the task at hand.

They walk home beneath telegraph wires stretched white across an ink-dark sky. Now and then they cross a pavement vent spewing steam into the freezing air. Neither say anything at first, then Sato asks: 'And what did you dream about today, Grandpa?'

There is a long pause, filled with the muffled sounds of village life, with the smell of dinners cooking.

'I dreamed of dumplings, Sato. I dreamed of Mrs Ikeda's dumplings. Let's see if the store is still open.'

They take a detour up to the high street. The boy walks his bicycle, bouncing it on and off the pavement while Tamamoto takes great care with each slippered step.

Tamamoto does not go to the onsen the following evening. The Americans are due at six and he has no idea how long it will all take. His daughter has prepared a huge amount of kitsune soba just in case. They've told him the documentary will be called *Survivors of Hiroshima*, which is about as good as any title, he thinks, for something beyond words.

Exactly on time, three young Americans turn up wheeling cases of equipment. There is the young woman. And there are two men. They seem school age. They are wearing T-shirts and jeans. One of the men is chewing gum. They make polite greetings then get to work and the little living room is soon ablaze with lights and reflectors. They sit him down and, in no time, the lens of a large mounted camera is pinning him to his armchair like a prize moth. He can feel the beads of sweat rolling down the back of his shirt.

Over the last seventy years, old Tamamoto had rarely spoken of his experience; now he finds himself candidly answering questions, sometimes through an interpreter who has turned up at the last minute, and sometimes without help. Some of the questions seem bizarre given the course of events. They are asked by the young woman, seated on a stool facing him. She is every bit as pretty as he remembers from her first visit. Her face is made-up. Her hair is very neat. A bare knee pokes through a hole in the denim of her trousers. She is constantly nodding and he appreciates that she is doing her best to be respectful. It comes back to him at last. Her name is Liv.

After what seems like an eternity, Liv finally comes to the last of her well-prepared questions:

'And, finally, Mister Tamamoto, do you have any regrets?'

'Does Oppenheimer have any?'

This is his well-prepared reply.

Tell us a bit about yourself

David Shelley Jones

She sits facing a computer screen at the back of the house in the room everyone calls the office. It is from here that her mother runs the business of the family farm. She is tense today. Her back is ramrod straight back, her forearms are resting on the oak desk at neat right-angles and her eyes are fixed dead ahead like a dog who has just spotted a rabbit.

The room is bulging with boxes and books and files and the sediment of generations: golf clubs, hockey sticks, photo albums, game boards and twenty years' worth of National Geographic that cannot be thrown out because they belonged to her mother's father. There is even a croquet set – a relic from the golden years when lawns were green and mowed, when Pimms was drunk on Sunday afternoons.

The room would be claustrophobic were it not for a large window looking out over the home paddock, the shearing sheds, and, in the distance, a faint line of dark blue hills. It is mainly flat, granite country – good soil when it rains; just dust in drought. The periods where money is made are brief. There is wheat in the good years and contracting work when things are desperate.

The farm carries three thousand sheep, give or take – depending on dingos, boundary losses, thieving, natural attrition, and random luck. Her father does the hands-on farming with just one full-time helper, Bob, who, truth be told, is past it. She had two brothers. Now she has one. Jim went off jackerooing, got into the booze, rolled his car near Wilcannia when he was only twenty-two. And there's Angus, working on an oil rig in the North Sea. Angus never gets in touch. Angus has a cold heart. Her mother has angina; so, it is up to her, Margot, the wonder girl, to take the overnight coach from Sydney when there's drenching or shearing on; or when her dad's back is playing up. It's a seven-hour trip. She does it every few months.

On the bare wall behind her are scattered small hooks and variations in paint tone suggesting the former presence of frames. Yesterday evening, her mother had taken down the family photographs, the award certificates, mainly prizes from when she was school dux, school captain, netball captain and just about everything else. Bella had advised her not to *give them any cues* – *them* being the people from the unfathomable world of the big organisation in the city she wants to join – *them* being the people who will interview her in a few minutes via Skype. Margot shuffles in her chair, rearranges the notes in front of her, takes a sip of water. They had better not be late she thinks, I'm psyched up. I cannot wait a moment longer.

A sound of spurting steam is coming from the hallway. Her mother has probably moved the ironing board closer to be within earshot. Her mother shares her ambitions.

‘Never you mind about us,’ she said when the possibility of a prestigious city job came up. ‘You’ve got to make your own way. Isn’t that right, Jock?’

It was after dinner several months earlier. Her father had his feet up in front of the TV. She knew she had to raise the subject before her father dozed off. He always dozed off around eight pm with a half-drunk stubby of beer on the coffee table in front of him. He’d start work at the crack of dawn. It was understandable.

‘Yeah,’ said her father. ‘She’s got to do what’s good for her.’ And for emphasis, ‘You’re a good girl, Margot, you just do what you want to do and don’t worry about us – we’ll manage well enough.’

And that was it. Her father never wasted words. Her father was the third generation on the farm and she, therefore, the fourth. The roots grow deeper.

She is well dressed to the level of her waist: white business blouse with a modest amount of make-up and hair done up in a bun – exactly the way Bella advised. Out of camera shot are dirty khaki shorts, a lucky platted leather belt and thin, long legs leading down to spotted socks. Her working boots are at the front door. It’s the spring uni break; just one more term at university before graduation – an arts/law degree with honours – as everyone expected. Margot delivers, Margot gets it done, she thinks, even if the price is bitten-down nails, sleepless nights and history of anorexia. She really wants this job. It involves helping people help themselves, which is her ideal.

The interview takes a few minutes to get underway because of poor reception. After some awkward verbal exchanges, a man and a woman materialise on the screen. They are about the age of her parents. The woman looks interested and possibly kind-hearted. The man seems bored. After brief eye contact and a ‘good morning, Margot’ he returns to looking down at something out of view.

The lady is in a business suit. She is wearing too much lipstick and her hair is surprisingly messy. There is a bookcase behind her laden with fat files in ring-binders. She tries to put Margot at ease with preliminary chit-chat about the airline strike and the drought. Then she says, ‘So, Margot, tell us a bit about yourself.’

Margot glances at her crib cards. She knows she must incorporate the following words in her reply: **diligent *passionate *curious *adaptable *resilient*.

Bella said, ‘Trust me on this, Margot, darling.’

Margot manages to include all the words in her reply, but there is no time for self-congratulation because the next question follows hard upon the first. Presumably, there are a lot of applicants. She wonders if they take it in turns to be ‘on the job.’ Clearly, it is the woman’s turn.

The woman asks her about the *Indian Project.* It is in her CV.

On the wall behind the screen, slightly to her right, is the word **INDIA** in bold black capitals on butcher’s paper. There are bullet points below, a column of single words preceded by asterisks: **stakeholders *respect* *ethics *cultural sensitivity *change.* She expertly weaves them into a description of her university project about solar power in Indian slums. She does not mention the difficulties faced by a tall, blonde white woman with an interpreter trying to tie down slum-dwellers with a long questionnaire. She doesn't talk about the challenges of promoting solar panels to people living under leaking, corrugated iron roofs. 'Keep everything positive,' that's what Bella said. 'You are lovely, the world is lovely; ergo, your words must be lovely.' If Margot is one of the current young stars of country NSW, then Bella is exalted alumni. Bella is nearing the end of a highly contested graduate program herself. 'You have to be holier than Jesus to get in,' Bella advised.

Next comes a hypothetical scenario about a tricky situation, a wicked problem as one of Margot's lecturers would call it. A crew member is very sick on a ship, having embarked with a slight fever. It is probably Ebola. There is a dilemma regarding isolation and the issue of compromising the ship's doctor and nurse. Margot wants to say that, being a countrywoman, she doesn't do hypotheticals, she just applies common sense on a case-by-case, moment-by-moment basis; but she doesn't – she refers to a cue card headed: *Any hypothetical question,* which is taped to a corner of her screen. The words **refer *consult *protocol *team-oriented* roll smoothly off her tongue. 'God, I'm a pro,' she thinks.

Finally, the inevitable 'working for us' questions arrive. This is on the butcher's sheet to Margot's left: **self-motivated *accountable *committed *collaborative.* Margot pauses for a moment, thinking that no one on earth can get so many buzzwords into so few sentences. Then she draws a short breath and a deluge of the right words roll naturally off her tongue – as fluently as her very good French.

'Thank you,' the interviewers say, 'we will be in touch late October.' The man was apparently paying attention at the end; surely, a good sign.

The screen goes blank. Margot stands up and stretches and asks the spider near the window, 'Well, Mr Daddy Long-Legs, how did I go?' Every muscle in her body begins to ease. She gets up and leaves the room to talk to her mother in the hallway. She sees that only one pillowslip has been ironed.

'How'd it go, love?' her mother asks, putting the iron down and searching her face for clues.

'Pretty good, I think…not bad…about what I expected.'

Margot goes to the kitchen and gets a beer and returns to continue talking to her mother, but her mother cuts her short.

'Dad's just been on the radio: he's wondering whether you can take the quad bike out to Wattle Creek with half a dozen star posts and the post driver. Also, wire from the back shed. Sorry, love – a tree's fallen across the fence and Bob's in town. I've got a nice roast going for you when you get back.'

****

The spot is twenty minute's ride away and her father already has a large casuarina in pieces by the time she arrives. Great slices of the dismembered tree lie scattered around a ragged hole in the fence. A cooling chainsaw rests on the back of the ute. Her father, now in his late fifties, a little paunchy in the belly, is sitting on one of the logs having a rest. His shirt is soaked in sweat, the front of which is dirty white, the back almost grey with flies. A few remaining strands of his once fine, dark head of hair are plastered across his forehead, mixed with sawdust and dirt. Margot marvels that he has done it all by himself. She worries for her Dad. She imagines him dying alone one day - out in the middle of nowhere. A heart attack, an accident. It happens.

'Lightning strike,' he says as she approaches. He seldom indulges in the luxury of verbs. She knows he means that the tree was weakened a while ago by lightning and now, finally, it has given up the ghost. She can see the tell-tale bits of charcoal amongst its ruins.

Then her father says, 'Thanks, Margot. Great girl!' and they unload the posts and the very heavy coil of smooth wire. The barbed wire has recoiled on either side of the hole like two halves of a cut snake. She knows he'll reuse the barbed wire. In all things, he is economical.

****

On the way home, she thinks about her life back in Sydney, about her boyfriend – or, probably, soon to be ex-boyfriend. James is smart, ambitious, muscled from early morning gym sessions; but he's not a real man, she thinks, not like her dad or her brother. James is a verbal warrior. He thrusts and parries with nouns and verbs – in a good way – to good purpose – it's understandable. What else is there in a city other than words? Being good at words herself, she knows that there is opportunity in the city. Somewhere, buried in the concrete and glass, there must be a treasure trove of success and fulfilment. That's the logic; but she finds the pull of open landscape hard to resist, the gravity of empty space. Something is compelling about a life lived largely without dialogue, a life unedited by intellectuals. It's in her blood, after all. And what is James? All talk, all city. If she's going to live in the city, she at least needs a man who has a bit of country in him, a bit of sky in his eyes. She remembers a recent foreshore walk in Sydney. She and James had only just begun when the weather changed and a thin curtain of light rain began falling across the scene before them – the purple bay, the sleepy federation houses, the pale eucalypts, the tidy, bobbing boats. Just as she was thinking how lovely it all was, James piped up and said: 'Let's go back, it's getting wet.' And then there was the fuss of dealing with muddy shoes in his new Audi.

When she is roughly halfway along the shortcut to the homestead, she finds a roo caught in the fence-line, its hind leg snared between two strands of overlapping wire – suspended at a terrible angle. The strangeness of this is unsettling – the most sure-footed of creatures – upside down – immobilised. She can tell by the matted fur, the arc of flattened dirt and grass, that the animal has been lying there for at least a day or two.

She dismounts and approaches the poor creature. The leg is broken, yet the animal is very quiet. Everything is very quiet. In the back blocks, late in the day, when the sun is setting behind the hills and there's no wind, the silence is almost absolute. The silence of the country distressed the early settlers. The Aborigines dealt with it. They talked. They sang. They moved about in song lines.

The roo is looking at her, not in terror, but with resignation. She can see the flecks of brown and blue in its eyes – and, also, the reflection of passing clouds. It is breathing quick, soft, shallow breaths.

She goes back to the quad and gets a skinning knife and stands by the roo with the silver blade catching the last of the sunlight. With her left hand, she draws its head gently backwards and with a single, swift stroke she cuts its throat and steps back, knife at her side, watching the creature's eyes grow dull, the ground darken around its neck.

She drags the roo clear of the fence and, realising that it is a female, checks the pouch. To her relief, there is no joey. Several hundred metres away, before a copse of she-oak, a big buck roo is watching. She knows the rest of the mob are also there, out of sight, waiting for nightfall; when they will return to sniff about and accept what is, what must be.

Walking back to the quad, she says softly: 'You want me to tell you a bit about myself? Well, this is a bit about myself.'

Traces

Amanda Hildebrand

The first time Caro noticed something was wrong, she was high in the air, eating mini pretzels and drinking white wine from a plastic cup. Her life played out in public spaces – featureless airport lounges, hole-in-the-wall cafés, city parks on sunny days – and she felt the encroachment upon them by staff cuts and malicious bits of street furniture as a kind of latter-day enclosure of the commons. There was no napping on a park bench anymore, jacket balled up beneath her head. Some train stations had done away with seating altogether, installing resting rails where commuters could lean for a few moments to take the weight off their office-shod feet before filing into the carriage. The aircraft cabin was one of the few places where the poorly defined crime of loitering did not apply, and so on the return flight from corporate client meetings, Caro often found herself concentrating less on work than the ballet of strangers, dancing for space in the aisles and on the armrests.

Caro had settled into her seat on one such return flight when it happened. She was snacking on pretzels and hummus, and fanning through the annual report she had just prepared for a supermarket chain. The man next to her seemed to be studying an advertisement for shoe lifts in the inflight magazine. He had lingered on the same page for several minutes; Caro watched sidelong, curious to see whether he would tear it out. She saw it fleetingly at first or rather gauged the lack of it, and her attention quickly returned to her reading material. She turned the pages of the report carefully, examining each full-colour photograph in an effort to confirm what her distracted glance had suspected. Her CEO-client had insisted that contractors be included in the division photographs, a gesture she had understood as the most visible expression the CEO could muster of his commitment to the firm's values statement, which mentioned something vague about treating stakeholders like family. Still, it had been a novelty for Caro, and she had dressed in her grey suit, had her hair done, and taken extra care over her makeup that morning. She was placed by the photographer at the end of one row, next to a man who wore large, sparkly red hearts as cufflinks, crafted by his daughter at after-school care. The man laughed with Caro about how the glitter shedding onto his business shirt made him look like a faded magician. They were laughing when the shutter clicked.

The photograph was there, in the marketing and communications section of the annual report. Three rows of stakeholders, smiling at the camera. There, in the middle row, was the man who had been placed next to her that day, brushing glitter from his shirt. On the outer edge of the row stood a woman Caro had never seen before. She consulted the legend, which informed her in a small, san-serif font, chosen for its cordiality, that the woman was Eliza Frank, Marketing Assistant. She was definitely not Caroline Dent, Corporate Communications Consultant. Caro drank the rest of her wine and splayed the report onto her tray table. The man in the middle seat tore the shoe lift advertisement from the inflight magazine and quickly pocketed a scrap of paper, but Caro barely registered the action. She scoured every face in the image before her twice, three times. The evidence was conspicuous by its absence. She had disappeared from the photograph.

There were several explanations. Perhaps another photograph had been taken on a different day, a day when Caro wasn't invited to the session? This seemed unlikely; the CEO was not known for extravagance beyond a certain, PR-friendly point. A quirk of the camera, then, or a glitch in the printing? But Caro knew the photographer; in fact, she had recommended him to the CEO. Still, as soon as she landed, Caro texted the photographer to ask if he recalled her being present on the day the picture was taken. He was adamant that she had not been at the shoot. It was reporting season, a busy time of year for them both, but despite their occasional spiky exchanges, she knew the photographer had a good eye for detail and was not prone to practical jokes. Caro doubted her recollection even less than that of the photographer, but in the interest of thoroughness she checked her diary: there was the appointment for the photoshoot. The tyranny of the freelancer's timesheet had gifted her with the habit of meticulous note-taking, and if her diary said she had attended a photoshoot that day, then she was prepared to believe it.

Caro was disturbed by the unexplained absence. It scratched at her faith in plans and outcomes. Her supermarket client kept a regional office a good two hours' drive from her home, but the roads were reasonable outside of peak hour, and the fuel consumption could be written off as a business expense. Caro made the round trip to the regional office, citing due diligence to the receptionist, who was used to complying with odd requests and rounded up each department's copy of the annual report without comment. Twenty minutes and twenty copies later, Caro was obliged to accept that she had gone missing from them all.

The walls of Caro's apartment were bare, except for the small Mondrian print hanging in her home office. The tight rectangles and confident primary colours kept the deadlines from crowding around her. Every other picture, every personal record, was archived on her hard drive. She booted up her laptop and, for what may have been the first time, scrolled through her collection of school photos and holiday snaps. She was exactly as she remembered, smiling out from foreign landmarks and birthday parties, weddings and graduations, save for that one, brief period when she fancied herself a melancholic and refused to be photographed. But that absence had boundaries, its own established place in Caro's narrative. This new, this other absence, isolated though it appeared to be, had by now become immense, distended in her mind. A small corner of her visual history had been erased, and there was no telling what it meant or whether it would stop, whether each record of her would splinter into fragments, the fragments into dust, the dust into air, air that moved to fill the space she had silently vacated.

****

Caro was in the lobby of a global banking behemoth, seated as straight-backed as she could tolerate in the low, marshmallow-soft lounge when she received the message that repaid her instincts about the new project. It had come about when she asked her photographer friend if he had any candid images of her, pictorial traces which might slip into oblivion unlabelled, unknown, even by Caro herself. The photographer sorted through his digital files and came up with a single picture, taken at least ten years ago, at what looked like a celebratory picnic. Neither of them recalled the occasion. Caro could barely accept that she once owned a denim jacket, but the picnic vignette before her insisted that she had, at least at one point in her past, been the sort of person who wears a denim jacket.

Caro and the photographer had been casual acquaintances at college, but it wasn't until they ran into each other on the corporate circuit that they truly connected. She liked the way he called her Caro, not Caroline, like the revival of a dead language, one that she had buried. They traded stories about clueless clients and outstanding balances and reminisced about the old days and old ambitions. She had been determined to write the next great novella – the slim volume, she had called it – he, to become a nature photographer. They consoled each other that they were at least practising their craft, unlike many of their college cohorts, but even as they spoke the words echoed in their ears.

It was the image of that stranger, a decade younger, dressed in a manner unfamiliar – undesirable – to the corporate Caro, that set the project in motion. It was not the slim volume she had intended, but amidst the product disclosure statements and web copy for catering companies and annual reports that concealed blunt challenges to her history, it was salvage work. Here, seated in the marble lobby of her new banking client, enjoying the free wi-fi and the mellow, burnt-caramel-coffee atmosphere wafting from the atrium café as she wrote up her meeting notes, her work began with a haptic buzz by her arm. She glanced from her notes to find a message glowing on the home screen of her phone:

Hi, our tour guide recommended this place for lobster soup. It was the first trip overseas for both of us. My boyfriend wouldn't touch the bread because he forgot his hand sanitiser. I'm not with him anymore, but not because of that. Not sure if this is what you want?

Caro clicked on the image below the message. A small, crowded restaurant materialised on her phone screen: a place with no particular aesthetic, cobbled together with communal benches and time-bleached timber stools and newspaper reviews taped to the walls, blemished and brittle from the daily coat of culinary steam that rose from the kitchen. To the left of the centre, two faces, one female, one male, smiled directly at the camera. The smiles appeared genuine, the faces a little weary – wary? – and perhaps not yet thirty. The frame was tight around them; the woman's arm formed a vector from the lens to her shoulder, which shrugged towards her ear, suggesting that she had taken the picture. The man's head tilted onto the woman's resting shoulder. Caro was struck by the quaintness of the composition, the woman's dominance of space and stance, how she seemed to extend from the frame into real space, while the man receded as if captured in the act of joining with the steam, shifting from matter to vapour. In the background, slightly to the right of the main pair, somewhat out of focus, sat a woman with wiry brown hair and a red beanie, her khaki all-weather jacket unzipped, red scarf looped, loose and casual, around her neck. She paid no attention to the nearby couple, concentrating instead on the bowl before her.

Caro knew that the photograph had been taken in Iceland. She remembered the rich, buttery taste of the lobster chunks, the thick saltiness of the broth, the heat from the bowl raising a flush on her face. She still had the all-weather jacket, although the scarf had been lost, somewhere in transit between Amsterdam and Berlin. This brief stop on her solitary journey through the glassy, winter-white Icelandic landscape, had become a cameo in the travel anecdotes of two maiden voyagers as they enjoyed their bowl of soup with her, they with their backs to her, before dispersing into the crowd, all three of them, spinning onto separate paths.

Caro saved the image to her phone. This was exactly what she wanted.

****

Caro's post, featuring a close-up of her smiling face, asking readers to send in images they had inadvertently taken of her, together with the story that framed the photograph for them, travelled far beyond her network.

This first photograph came from a stranger who had unwittingly shared soup with Caro. The second, from a neighbour who had captured her feet, clad in wellington boots, as she walked past the neighbour's tulip garden. The project began to gather momentum, planting distance between Caro and that still-smarting point at which she confronted the image that denied her, replaced her, buried deep within the pages of a pedestrian report. People seemed to relish the opportunity to connect their stories to hers, to relive them through revealing to her the literal bigger picture, the events in which she had shared without ever knowing it.

There was Caro, riding a friend's bike past the lens of an architect who had been surveying a vacant lot. She mingled with the crowd at a conference, chatting to the keynote speaker, who remembered their excited conversation about kaleidoscopes, their favourite childhood toy. She was spotted on a quiet country lane, walking past a roadside memorial.

The messages that accompanied the images, these narratives in which she had played her part in ignorance, ranged from the mundane to the bittersweet, to the unexpected:

We were at the National Gallery to settle an argument about a Van Gogh self-portrait. We didn't know it was in the Rijksmuseum. We owed each other a coffee! We were just heading in as you were heading out if that's you at the bottom of the steps.

There you are, watching us leap about trying to get a taxi. It was about 2, so pretty hammered by then. There was track work, so we slept outside the station till it opened Mon morn.

I went to Borough Market, especially for the cheese toasties. Pretty sure I'd seen you there before, how cool is that! BTW, I have an Instagram about cheese. Follow me?

I was taking a picture of my dog chasing a stick. I didn't really see you walking towards me when I was taking the photo, but I remember my pop spilt a thermos of tea on the picnic blanket straight after I took it. Did you see that? He has Parkinson's Disease. Did you hear what my dad said to him? They won't tell me.

Caro sent the dozens of images she had received to her photographer colleague. She didn't admit to what had inspired the idea, but he knew enough about her to guess and to be concerned that he was indulging something that flourished from a mistake or memory lapse, that turned a bland photograph in an annual report, designed to be glanced over, into something else, weighted with substance. Nevertheless, he liked Caro's concept and the promise of creativity that reporting season did not permit, and he turned over to her the small, white cube gallery he had leased to exhibit his nature photography. Together, they printed, framed and hung each image, alongside the texts that accompanied them. When the show was ready to open, Caro slipped discreetly away. She had the feeling that she shouldn't be there, shouldn't chance meeting any of her correspondents in this stark space, unreal and distinct from life as it was. In place of her body, she left the unremarkable photograph of the marketing and communications department of a supermarket chain, the one that had lost her likeness. A four-word label was fastened to the wall beside it:

Not pictured: Caroline Dent

White Angel

Paul Chiswick

A small flotilla of boats bucks wildly on the choppy waters of St Mary's Pool. In the near distance, Samson rises up, barely visible in the squall. On the street a handful of people lean into the wind, hands gripping hoods, anoraks glistening.

Rowena peers through the hotel bedroom's rain-slashed window, the wind whistling eerily through its ill-fitting frame. She is tempted to kneel, clasp hands and pray to God the filthy weather will continue. This is the place she hoped never to see again. Forty-one years ago, these islands snatched her beloved Oliver from her. For forty-one years she has avoided them.

'I found this on the internet, Mum.'

Rowena turns away from the window. Seated on the edge of the bed, Lucy, her daughter, unfolds a sheet of paper.

'What is it?'

'A copy of a newspaper article. I think you should read it before we catch the boat tomorrow.'

'Would you mind reading it to me? My head feels like the inside of a drum after the ferry.'

'It's from *The Times*, dated 15th August 1979.'

Rowena's stomach tightens.

Lucy begins to read: 'The Fastnet race has been held every year since 1925, except during the war. It is a classic amongst offshore races. Starting at Cowes on the south coast, it goes around the Fastnet Rock off the coast of Ireland and finishes at Plymouth, a distance of 605 miles. The race has an excellent safety record…'

'Stop, please. No more!'

Rowena presses her fingers to her temples. Sucks in a lungful of air. An original cutting of the article gathers dust in her writing bureau, out of sight, but never out of mind.

'Why, Lucy? Why are we here?'

'You know why. You agreed it's time you laid Dad's ghost to rest.'

'I…I may have made a mistake. Can we do this another time?'

Lucy rises from the bed. Draws herself up to her full height, towering over her mother. She crosses her arms over her chest, stretches her mouth in a tight line.

'When? Next week? Next year?'

'Please, my head…'

'You're a coward, Mum. All I'm asking you to do is take a boat trip to see where he lost his life. Is that too much to ask?'

'Darling, I can't… I can't…'

'You can. You promised me.'

Rowena reaches into her handbag, pulls out a tissue and balls it in her fist.

'Must we do this, Lucy? Can't we just turn around and go home?'

'No, we can't. You're not the only one who carries this particular monkey on her back, you know.'

'But I don't see how Oliver's…' the word doesn't want to come out, 'death affected you so much. You were only five at the time.'

'Hughie found this on my bedside table. He couldn't understand why we haven't been to see where Dad died. I really didn't know what to tell him.'

Rowena's grandson is sixteen, strapping, sailing mad. He hopes to represent Great Britain in the men's one-person dinghy in the 2024 Olympics. Very proud of his grandfather, Lucy tells Rowena, although Hughie has never mentioned Oliver to Rowena. She supposes Lucy has told him to tiptoe carefully around his grandmother's emotions.

'He's more mature than his years, Mum. He's very good at looking at things from more than just one viewpoint. He says the sea can be forgiving as well as cruel.'

The only image of the sea Rowena can conjure up is an angry maelstrom dashing itself against razor-sharp rocks, black and sulphurous, Oliver's yacht pitching and rolling its fragile backbone snapped in two.

Words rush out before she can stop them. 'Does he? And he would know, would he? I wouldn't be surprised if he ends up like Oliver!'

Lucy's cheeks flush crimson. Rowena steps forward, a sudden need to enfold her daughter in her arms. Lucy's raised palms, fingers splayed like starfish, stop her.

'I'll put that outburst down to your headache. I'm going for a bath. We can discuss this again over dinner.'

'The Last Supper?' says Rowena.

'For pity's sake!' Lucy spins on her heels and strides out of the room.

Rowena awakes to find sunlight lancing through a gap in the curtains. Bright red figures on the bedside clock declare the time is 8:52. The smell of bacon frying hangs in the air. Mildly disorientated, she cannot recall why the window is on the left side of the bed and why there should be the sound of laughter outside it. Then it dawns on her where she is.

A light tapping on the door. 'Are you awake, Mum?'

She jams her fist in her mouth, squeezes her eyes tight shut.

Knuckles attack the door like an angry woodpecker. 'Mum! Are you there?'

'Is something the matter?' another voice, more distant, concerned, unsure.

'No, it's nothing. My mother is…a little hard of hearing, that's all.'

‘Well, if you wouldn’t mind hurrying her along. We finish serving breakfast at nine-thirty.’

‘Yes, sorry.’

The whisper floats through the keyhole like poison gas: ‘Don’t be so childish, Mum. The boat leaves at eleven. There’s no way you won’t be on it.’

When Eleanor enters the cramped dining room Lucy is sitting at a table in conversation with a woman whose mouth reveals a perfect set of dentures, much too large for it. Lucy scowls and points at the chair next to hers. Rowena feels like an errant child as she edges around the tables, forcing a smile on the seated guests.

‘This is your mother, I gather,’ says the woman. As Rowena takes her place, the woman holds out her hand and clacks, ‘Ruby Tremayne. Pleased to meet you.’

‘Eleanor. Eleanor Magnusson.’

Sharing a table with a stranger is not Rowena’s idea of fun. Any minute now this woman will tell her what an unusual name she has; she is sure she has heard it before; it seems to ring a bell.

‘Magnusson? What an unusual name. I’m sure…’

‘Full English?’ A teenage girl slouches at the edge of the table, weight on one leg, face blank with boredom. A black skirt barely covers her backside and there is an egg stain on the front of her white blouse.

Rowena could not digest food even if her stomach reached out of her mouth and dragged it in.

‘No, thank you. I’m not hungry.’

‘Tea? Coffee? Juice?’

‘A glass of water would be fine.’

The girl looks at Rowena as if she might be ET, and Rowena is tempted to ask if she can phone home, because at this precise moment that is exactly where she wants to be.

‘Beautiful day.’ Ruby’s face beams at Rowena. ‘Lucy tells me you’re taking a little trip out to the Western Isles.’

A tic triggers in Rowena’s eyelid.

‘I’ve never been there myself, but I do hear they are so wondrously mysterious. Mind you, you don’t want to get too close to that nasty Bishop Rock.’

A cold finger traces the curve of Rowena’s spine.

‘The forecast is for fair weather,’ Lucy says quickly. ‘Probably be as calm as a millpond.’

‘Ain’t never calm, never,’ snaps the girl. She holds out her hand, shows an ugly red scar that runs from the base of her little finger to the fleshy mound of her thumb. ‘Got that on Bishop Rock. Could have been much worse. Dead lucky I were.’

Lucy glances at her watch. ‘Time to go, Mum.’

'The Last Supper is done with, now the crucifixion?' says Rowena.

Ruby and the girl stare at her, their eyebrows knotted like spaghetti.

A dozen feet below the quayside, a line of boats waits patiently, diesel engines putt-putting. A bustling woman with a clipboard directs visitors to craft for St Agnes, Bryher, Tresco, and St Martin's.

Foul weather has hammered the islands for the past week. Not today. Today is a day tripper's dream.

'There's our boat,' says Lucy. 'Let's go.'

She clamps her hand on Rowena's forearm and hauls her to where a green and cream boat nestles between much more solid neighbours. Its wheelhouse, set aft, seems barely big enough to hold one person. An uncovered deck affords no protection from the elements.

Rowena shrugs off Lucy's hand. 'You can't be serious. If you think I'm setting foot on that, you've another thing coming.'

'The chap comes highly recommended, Mum. There's nothing to worry about.'

'The boat is far too small for Rowena's liking. The last time she was on water was a Nile Cruise. Three decks up, she could have been in a five-star hotel, there was so little movement. And there were no crashing breakers on the Nile.

'But look at it! If a big wave hits that thing, it's bound to capsize!'

'Oh, so you know all about boats now? Come on, mind the steps.'

Rowena treads gingerly on the weathered concrete steps, holding on to a filthy rope that passes through iron eyelets driven into a harbour wall fringed with dark seaweed smelling of roasted nuts and iodine and scaly with barnacles.

'Careful, missus, the step's a mite slippery.'

The boatman's calloused hand grasps Rowena's in a firm grip. She looks up into a face etched with fine tracery like a spider's web. Green eyes peer from under brows the colour of cigarette ash. The man has dressed for the part: blood-red Dutch Fisherman's cap, faded black sweatshirt, heavy brown corduroys and roped-soled shoes. As she steps warily onto the boat's varnished deck, she feels it rock. The boatman's other hand gently cups her elbow.

'Steady, there! We don't want any accidents.'

Lucy arranged this trip a month ago. Ever since, Rowena's nerves have been as taut as piano wires. Her poor fingernails are chewed almost to the quick. She should have stood firm; told Lucy she is not yet ready to face her demons. Now it is too late. Now they're here and in less than an hour, they will be *there*. Not a day passes without her heart somersaulting when she thinks of the daring, devil-may-care husband she had for such a short time. She keeps her memories private, hides them away in her grief-filled locker, secretes them even from Lucy.

'This is not a good idea, Lucy,' Rowena hisses.

Face impassive, Lucy says nothing.

The boatman eases the throttle forward. The little craft jerks into life, its bow rising. From where Rowena sits, she can see the sickle sweep of Town Beach and the white-walled, grey-roofed houses of Hugh Town crowding the water's edge. Lucy takes a book out of her handbag – *Isles of Scilly Guidebook* – flicks through it and stops at a page titled *Getting your bearings on Scilly* that shows a stylised map. Rowena tries not to look but cannot resist. Her eyes flit westwards past St Mary's, The Gugh, St Agnes, Annet, finally stopping where the print almost bleeds off the page.

She freezes. There it is. The size of a full stop. Bishop Rock.

The boatman trims the throttle. The engine settles into a steady beat. He bends down and then steps out of the wheelhouse, clasping an orange life jacket in each hand.

'Best if you wear these,' he says, 'case you goes overboard. Name's Gabriel, like the angel.'

Lucy points at Rowena, then herself. 'Rowena. Lucy.'

'Welcome aboard the *Pride of Bryher*.'

Beads of sweat bubble on Rowena's forehead. 'The forecast is for good weather, isn't it?'

'So 'tis, missus, but these waters can change faster'n a chameleon. My advice would be to put this on. If you don't want to, you don't have to. It's your choice.'

The jacket is bulky, uncomfortable, chafing Rowena's neck. It feels as if it has been forced into a child's turtleneck sweater.

'Ain't nothin' as beautiful as the Western Rocks on a calm day,' booms Gabriel's voice. 'If you looks to your left over there, that's Annet we're passing.'

Lucy takes Rowena's hand in hers and pats it. 'Relax, Mum. Won't be long now.'

'Seal at nine o'clock.' On the port side of the boat, Gabriel points to where the disembodied head of a grey seal breaks through the sea's silvery skin. As they watch more heads pop up, a whole colony – bulls, cows and calves – eyeing them as they chug past. It strikes Rowena they are the watchers, not her.

'Aren't they beautiful?' Lucy trains her camera on the curious animals. As she does so, two oily backs silently part the water not twenty yards away.

'Porpoises,' says Gabriel. 'And look there – you don't often see that – a pair o' shearwaters.'

Two black and white birds glide past and settle on a finger of rock. Behind them, a row of larger birds, green as dark seaweed, stand like sentinels.

'What are those?' Lucy asks.

‘Cormorants. Last year’s young. By this time next year, they’ll be jet black.’

Rowena feels the tension ease slightly as the scene draws her in. Only the occasional plopping sound of the seals, as they emerge and submerge, breaks the silence. She turns to face the bow and her heart almost stops. Rising straight and tall above her in all its white and towering splendour: Bishop Rock lighthouse.

Gabriel steps over and stands next to her, the tang of wool mixed with engine oil catching her nostrils. ‘Magnificent, ain’t she? Unmanned now, of course.’

Waves lick at the rock. Rowena cranes her neck to spot the lantern high above her. The structure is commanding, imperious, indefatigable.

‘The sea’s sleepin’,’ Gabriel says. ‘The old lighthouse, she’ll try her best to make sure the tricky old devil don’t take anyone unawares. Mind you, sometimes he catches her out.’

His words roll around Rowena’s head. Is that what happened that fateful year? Had *she* been caught out and failed to warn Oliver and his crew of impending danger?

‘My father died here. In the Fastnet,’ says Lucy.

Gabriel's eyes lock on hers. 'You talkin’ about the Grimaldi?’

Rowena clamps her hand over her mouth. The name haunts her, too close to grim, grimace, Grim Reaper.

‘A bad do, that. The sea was angry that day,’ he says. ‘I was right here in ’79. When it happened.’

Rowena’s eyes fly open. ‘In the lighthouse?’

‘I weren’t in the lighthouse. I was in a helicopter.’

‘A helicopter?’

‘Aye. At the time I were in the RNAS, based at Culdrose. We mobilised as part of the rescue effort. Directed to assist a yacht in trouble close by Bishop Rock.’

‘The Grimaldi.’ The name spills out before Rowena realises.

‘The very same.’

‘Did you…did you see what happened?’

Gabriel tugs his chin as if the memory lies beneath its skin. 'As much as I could, given the conditions.’

‘Tell me.’

‘We received a report from a vessel of this yacht bein’ tossed like a cork by a gigantic storm. The crew were tryin’ to outrun it, but it kept knockin’ the poor boat flat time after time, like it were swattin’ a fly, hurlin’ the sailors into the sea and to the end of their safety-line harnesses. The next we heard, a huge wave had flipped the yacht over and on to its back, dismastin’ it.’

‘And then it broke upon the rock?’

‘No missus, not when we got there. I heard that were later after we'd rescued as many of the crew as we could.’

‘You didn’t lift them off the rock, then?’

‘Lift them off the rock? Listen, we couldn’t get anywhere near it. The crew had inflated their life raft and then abandoned the boat when she capsized. That’s where we found them –in their lifeboat.’

‘All of them?’

‘No. They said the captain had been swept overboard by a breaker and carried away.’

‘He didn’t die on the rock?’

‘No missus, he didn’t.’

Rowena slides to the deck. Lucy wraps her arms around her, tears streaming down her face. Rowena doesn’t know if she should feel anger or relief. How cruel that poor Oliver was the only casualty on that fateful day. Yet, truth is, it was not Bishop Rock, the object of horror she has carried with her all these years, that took his life from him.

‘Thing is,’ says Gabriel, ‘if it hadn't been for the old lighthouse, we wouldn't have found any of them. Not a chance. She showed us the way that day, all right. That's why the seamen around here call her White Angel.’

The *Scillonian* cuts through the water, Hugh Town shrinking in its frothy wake. For the first time last night, Rowena did not dream of Oliver, his body lying broken and bloody on Bishop Rock.

Lucy’s hand squeezes hers. ‘It’s over, Mum. Time to move on.’

Rowena returns the squeeze. ‘Thank you, darling. For insisting I came.’

2020 RAINBOW PRIZE

Rainbow Prize Judge's Report

Leigh Russell

Judging the rainbow short story competition was a wonderful reading experience for me, but quite a headache in terms of judging, because the standard of writing was so high throughout. Just about every submission was brilliantly written. There were beautifully crafted phrases, wonderfully evocative descriptions, moving stories of tragic relationships, and amusing stories that really were very entertaining. I assessed the submissions on the quality of writing, idea, structure, plot, and characterisation. There was very little to criticise in any of the stories on the grounds of quality of writing. Each one was a joy to read. Eventually, with difficulty, I selected a long list of 20, which I then reduced to a shortlist of six from which I picked a winner, second and third place. They are worthy winners in a very strong field.

My third place choice is *Starlings*, which is well written and moving. This is a powerful story and the writer demonstrates great potential, but I did feel she tried to do too much for a short story. I felt this story was crying out to be a full-length novel. In second place, I chose *A Different Version.* This story was close to my heart being a crime story. It was well written with a slick plot twist, and a huge amount was achieved in a very short story.

And finally, in first place, comes *Memories from Muskwa Creek*. Here is a writer who understands how to show not tell. The reader is taken right into the scene, it becomes very real, and so are the characters, including the grizzly. This is powerful writing, vivid, authentic, and very convincing. The tension is brilliantly built throughout with a conclusion that is both subtle and unpredictable. A worthy winner.

WINNER

Memories from Muskwa Creek

Shirley Smith Matheson

Gus will know what's in the box. He'll read the postmark and, just like that, he'll see the river, the mine, the shack and the bear. The tawny fur is dull and moth-chewed, but the four-inch claws retain their majesty. The brass plaque, fronting the mahogany base on which the souvenir is mounted, simply states *Muskwa Creek, Alaska, August 12, 1962.*

I left a foster home in Seattle at sixteen and worked my way on a freighter up the Inside Passage to Alaska. On docking at Wrangell, I left the ship. The village was beautiful, with signs everywhere referring to its gold-rush history.

I entered a cafe and ordered a meal. One old-timer glanced at me and tipped his hat, so I nodded. He came over and pulled out a chair. 'What brings you here, young fella?'

I said I'd just disembarked from a freighter and asked if there was any work around here for a young guy. He laughed. 'You're a bit late for the gold, son, if that's what you're after. The Stikine Rush was sixty, seventy years ago. I was a kid then, but I remember all the stories. Wrangell was the shoving-off point for the Klondike gold fields up the Stikine River.

'There's still gold in the creeks, though, if you want to work for it,' he added. 'Those three gents over there are getting ready to go. You should talk to them.'

He wished me luck and left, while I sat wondering if I dared approach them. They were rather rough-looking chaps and seemed to be in a bit of an argument amongst themselves. But I was a risk-taker, so I went over and introduced myself.

'I just came from Seattle, on the freighter,' I said. 'I thought I might stick around, see what's going on. The old fellow told me you were outfitting for a trip to the goldfields.'

'Ain't no goldfields,' one fellow said. 'Just mining the creeks. Tough work…for men.' He looked at me, noting my size, nearly six feet tall, and strong from working on the farms that had supported the foster home.

'Got any money?' one asked.

'Some.'

They looked at each other and one introduced himself as Gus. 'This here's Sly and that's Gerard.' They nodded and indicated a chair for me to join them.

I became excited as they described their plans to prospect near the headwaters of the Lachish River. When I asked if they might take on a fourth partner, they exchanged glances, nods, and then Gus said, 'You'd have to put in twenty-five percent for expenses, maybe more if needed.'

I agreed.

'A gentleman's bond,' Sly said. 'Nothing in writing. Everyone puts in dough, shares the work and the profits. If no profits, tough luck for all.'

I checked out my new partners. Gus looked to be in his mid-twenties, fat and pink-skinned from sunburn, with a fringe of wiry red hair that horseshoed his balding head. Sly was around the same age, with a mass of black hair, a beard to match, and dark, brooding eyes. Gerard, likely in his late teens and youngest next to me, was small-built and quiet, with a nervous twitch. And then there was me, Theo Carr, an orphan, a kid from nowhere, ready for adventure.

We bought an old wooden riverboat and a Merc kicker from a prospector who was *gettin' the hell out*. With the old man dolefully watching us from the dock, we loaded our groceries and other supplies and then we four greenhorns sailed into uncharted wilderness.

I'd never seen anything like the Lachish...ice-white water laden with glacial silt, calm and fast-flowing until plunging over rock-strewn rapids and down steep falls. On our third night out, we camped on a narrow plateau at the river's edge and watched our firelight shoot eerie shadows up the granite face of the canyon wall behind us.

Gus was talkative, a good storyteller, but his main goal seemed to be to scare 'the kid.' As the flames from our campfire danced skyward, he related tales heard from local natives about flesh-eating Wendigo creatures. 'They stalk travelers.' He leaned toward me, pointing his fire stick. 'Scraps of corpses and clothing are found on trails, in cabins...nowhere is safe, if you're stalked by a Wendigo.' The men nodded solemnly or made grunting assents, but I laughed at his stories. When one of his tales seemed especially unbelievable, I spoke up. 'That's a lie – you dreamt it up!' The words erupted before I could stop them.

Gus glowered at me and abruptly ended his storytelling. He hadn't shown much liking for me before, and now I knew I'd made an enemy.

'Go fetch some driftwood, Theo,' Gus snapped. 'There's a pile down on the gravel bar.'

I cut through bushes to the river's edge, dropped down a three-foot cut bank, and backtracked to where Gus had spotted the wood. I was making my way along the rocky shoreline when I heard a noise. I stood still, wondering if I'd imagined it. When I threw my wood and ax up onto the ledge and started scrambling up the bank, a boot suddenly clamped down onto my right hand. I grabbed for my ax with my left hand, but it was wrenched from me and flung into the bush.

'You and me got some things to settle,' Gus said in a low voice. 'Like who calls the shots on this show.'

I was in good shape, but Gus had the advantage of higher ground, anger, and a hunting knife. He jumped down the graveled bank, and landed on top of me, kneeling on my chest and whipping my head around with furious boxing-ring punches. His red face, hovering inches from mine, showed rage and madness as he held the knife to my left ear, and sliced. 'A souvenir,' he said.

I cried out but no one came to my rescue.

Later, I lay partly submerged in the ice-cold river until the bleeding stopped and my senses returned. Then I wrapped my shirt around my head for a bandage and curled up under a bush on the graveled bank. When dawn came, I returned to the campsite. Neither Sly nor Gus looked at me, but Gerard silently pointed to some bacon in the pan and a portion of bannock left for me. I ate. There was no going back alone.

We boated and portaged our way further into the wilderness, with Sly and Gerard showing me a bit of slack and Gus ignoring me completely. My ear healed, but I couldn't see how badly it had been cut, only feel for what was left of it.

On our fifth night, while camping at the river's edge about thirty miles from our proposed destination, we heard a groan. Everyone went still.

'Quiet,' Sly said. 'It might come again.'

We scraped our coals into a heap and sat watching the salmon fry and the bannock brown in the pan. The sound came again – a long pain-filled moan that matched my own mood. I grabbed my ax and gun and crouched with my back against a big balsam fir. The others jumped up, rifles ready, but we heard only the wind in the trees, the low hoot of an owl, and the rolling hum of the river.

Over the next few nights, we heard the sound again and again. The farther the 'thing' tracked us, the more cruelly Gus treated me, as if I had become the cause. When we had to line the boat from the shoreline, I was made to pull from the toughest angle, often wading waist-deep in the cold river and stumbling over the boulder-strewn riverbed.

Nearly every night we heard the 'thing' cry: from the forest; from behind a rock-face; from across the river. We couldn't track it, we couldn't see it, and so we tried to ignore it.

Gus had some knowledge of woodlore but was clumsy and temperamental. He stumbled on slippery river stones, cracking his knee. As I watched him flail about on his bum leg and become increasingly cranky and helpless, my hatred for the man grew with every mile.

Sly was capable, but he wasn't much for teamwork. Gerard had the most wilderness knowledge but was uncommunicative and his nervous twitch was becoming worse.

At Sable Canyon, rock cliffs closed the riverbed to a narrow gorge and white water pounded like the maelstroms of hell. We were forced to portage and pull the boat and supplies overland on a narrow rock-strewn goat trail.

We had just made it past the canyon and were dropping down to the river when the cries came again, resounding off the rocks.

'A trapper disappeared right here, last winter,' Gus said as he painfully lowered his weight onto a fallen log and stretched out his stiff leg. 'Never found hide nor hair of him. Just a boot and his ax.'

'Probably a grizzly,' Sly said.

Gus nodded. 'He could have got caught in the canyon. Or went through the ice.'

I said nothing, having learned that silence was best around these volatile men.

The groans reverberated against the rock wall. The thing was either on the trail behind us or on the trail before us, for there was no other place to be. We made a small campfire and kept our loaded rifles handy.

'It's gotta be a bear,' Sly said, breaking his usual silence.

'Must be,' Gerard agreed. 'No human could sound like that.'

I ventured a suggestion: 'Why don't we set a trap, shoot it, and get it over with?'

Gus sneered. 'Maybe someone *did* shoot it. Likely got away on them. Bears don't wait around for the next bullet.'

'A bear cries when it's hit with a bullet,' Gerard said quietly. 'It bawls like a baby.'

'It's just a *bear*!' Gus said, spitting into the fire. 'No loss.'

But these sounds didn't resemble those of a bear, or a wolf, or a man. They resonated with despair, dementia, and terrible pain.

When dawn came, we broke camp and hit the trail. The cries followed, even as we branched off the Lachish River and navigated up Muskwa Creek. When we came upon a deserted trapper's cabin, it was decided that would be our summer home. The place stunk of pack rats, but we cleaned it out as well as we could and stored our supplies. Gus threw his bedroll on the elevated boards in one corner that the former owner had set up for a bed. Sly, Gerard, and I chose to sleep outside in hammocks or sheltered 'wickiup' lean-tos.

The next morning, we worked together on building a sluice-box and assigned rotating shifts: shoveling gravel, sluicing it down with water, and panning the black sand. Sly controlled the gravity feed system for the water, while Gerard and Gus shoveled. I helped at whatever job was assigned and did most of the cooking and cleanup. I was glad to be away from them, for almost immediately the men began to argue.

'For God's sake get a move on, Gus! We don't want to be stuck here till winter!' Sly said.

Gus nodded, sweat pouring off his head and trickling down his face and neck. His knee had become infected and looked bad.

Gerard and Sly worked all day, then washed up in the creek and came back to eat at a makeshift table fronting the cabin.

The work was backbreaking and endless. One day I dumped out some concentrates and the men exploded. 'You've thrown away half our profits, right there!' Gus yelled.

'There was no color left!' I said. 'You'd panned it already.'

'What would you know?' Sly muttered.

Gerard's face became dark as he banged his shovel around.

They're going to kill me, I thought. Either me or each other.

It stayed daylight until late in the evenings, when we sat around the campfire listening to the moans that floated through the still night air, challenging the Northern Lights for lunacy. It wore everyone down, working all day and then tossing about, sleepless, on rough spruce-bough beds or hammocks. The noise either blended with the sound of falling rain or was swept closer by the wind. It was impossible to pinpoint its direction. We feared the sound and we feared its absence. I constantly kept my .300 Savage with me, even while panning. I was prepared to use it on anything that threatened to attack, animal or human, and said so. Over the summer I'd become a crack shot.

'I saw some grizzly tracks,' Gerard said unexpectedly one night. 'Yesterday, when I shot the deer. Some measured ten inches across.'

We stared at him. We'd seen a track or two but they'd appeared to be old. If Gerard had spotted fresh tracks, why hadn't he said so earlier?

The next day the men trekked down to the diggings, leaving me home to dress out Gerard's deer. I cut and hung the quarters in trees to keep the meat away from animals, and had just returned to clean up the camp when I heard a moan. I stood still. There were no other sounds – no birds, no wind, no rustle of leaves or grass. I started toward the cabin to fetch my rifle that I'd left propped against the doorframe.

Then, I saw her.

She came from behind the cabin, an enormous grizzly, lurching like a drunkard through the salmonberry bushes. Something was dreadfully wrong. On gaining my scent, she reared up, and from the side of her twisted mouth came a bellowing roar. She fell back down on all fours and stumbled toward me. Her nearness was terrifying. I circled the trees to get to my rifle before she charged.

Suddenly, I noticed a movement in back of her. Gus was coming up from the creek, limping, looking down at his mutilated leg, self-centered as usual, and forgetting caution.

I'd never felt such a thrill in my life. It was her, or him, or me. The bear was horribly deformed, I could see that, and in pain. She was liable to attack at any moment. Which way she'd swing was the question.

I edged around a big pine. The bear swung her giant head in my direction, and then swooped back the other way as if searching for the foe. I realized she was blind in one eye. I slowly circled to her blind side, knowing smell was her sharpest sense and there was no wind to indicate my position.

Slowly, slowly I circled, careful to not snap a twig or make any sound or movement that might spring her into action. Twenty feet…now ten. Gus broke through the trees. The bear stood still, moaning softly, swinging her great head. She stunk like death.

Gus suddenly lifted his head and saw us, the bear swaying drunkenly, turning her lopsided head from him to me and back again; me with my .300 Savage loaded and aimed toward him and the bear, both within range.

She reared up, snarling crookedly from her twisted jaw. I had a split second to get my rifle up and one shot fired. She fell back and I pumped in another, then a third.

I sat down on a tree stump, afraid to advance in case she wasn't dead, or Gus was. The men, hearing the shots, came running from the creek.

Sly walked over to look at the brown hulk. 'Congratulations, kid,' he said. 'A clean kill.'

Gus lay on the ground, moaning, eerily picking up the tone and cadence of the old bear's cries. No one seemed to notice him as he crawled across the grass toward us. But I saw the fear in his eyes, the tears smeared on his cheeks with no attempt made to hide his fright.

'You did her a favor, Theo,' Gerard said, indicating the bear's twisted jaw, the missing eye. 'Hunters made a real mess of her.'

One eye and part of the bear's head had long ago been shot away and had healed in an infected mass of proud flesh. When we dressed her out, we found every kind of bullet in her made by man. A thick piece of snare wire was wrapped around one foot, nearly severing her paw.

'She was out of her mind,' Gerard said. 'You ended her misery, is all.'

'You'll make a good bushman one day,' Sly said.

'I'm sorry, kid,' Gus said.

I looked at him, sweat-stained, gaunt, and ill, his knee a mass of infection; a cruel man, a haunted man, a violator. I looked back at my bear.

Later, I had the paw of that old grizzly mounted, even though the sight of it still makes my breath catch.

Over the years I've often wondered what, in the end, I gained from that summer so long ago. The ultimate reward of survival? The memory of the split-second choice I made when I aimed my shot? The moment of maturity when I made my own peace in the wilderness?

The paw rests in the packing box ready to post and, for an instant, the fur glows bronze in the light reflected from the fireplace. The rusted wire retains its stranglehold on the paw, causing the claws to splay, fighting entrapment. The thing is now old, and rock-hard, like me. I close the lid and seal the box.

I know Gus is still alive although he must be nearly ninety now. He'll stare in shock at the postmark, *Wrangell, Alaska*, and he'll remember. He won't want to, but he'll open the package and there will be the paw. Images and sounds will crash through his mind: the wild water of the Lachish, the mine on Muskwa Creek, the pain endured for long-spent gold, the haunting tales of Wendigos, the stricken mutilated bear. And then, of course, he'll remember me.

SECOND PLACE

A Different Version

Janet Newman

Someone coughed and two black crows took off from the branch of a nearby yew tree. The handful of mourners lifted their heads in unison and watched the startled birds as they dipped and swooped over rows of faded headstones.

'I am the resurrection and the life,' the vicar intoned, bringing eyes back to the graveside, and heads to their former respectful positions.

Only Maureen continued to observe the crows. She watched them skew and glide and spread their wings to catch the wind and hover, for a heartbeat, before coming in to land again. They touched down – first one and then the other – onto a neighbouring mound, fresh-shovelled and offering up a wealth of hidden delights. More cocky than fearful now, the birds began to strike at the clayey loam as if they would pick bare the bones that lay beneath. And, all the time they stabbed and jabbed, Maureen watched and, as she watched, the hammer inside her chest boomed a thunderous accompaniment. The longer she watched, the more violent the beat became. Her head began to spin, the scene blurred, and she would surely have fallen, were it not for the steadying hand at her elbow. Maureen felt the fingers tighten and sensed, rather than saw the, *told you so,* look in her daughter's adolescent eyes. *Didn't I warn you,* the look would say. *Didn't I tell you to go easy on the hard stuff.*

But really, the girl knew. They both knew: Maureen could not have faced this day sober.

'We therefore commit his body to the ground...'

She snatched a lungful of air, told herself it would soon be over and resolutely switched her attention from the crows to the proceedings at the graveside.

The coffin was beginning its slow descent into the gaping earth.

'...earth to earth...'

Maureen tried hard to focus on Reverend Timmins' words. But a fragment of melody crept into her head and kept cutting across what he was saying.

'...ashes to ashes,' the vicar droned.

Killing me... a voice sang in her head.

'...dust to dust,' he said.

...softly, the song went.

Killing me softly.

In the early days, she and Steve had clashed over that number; argued about which artist performed it best.

'Roberta Flack,' Maureen insisted, 'no contest.'

But Steve had discovered another recording. A different version. By some little-known group whose name she couldn't even recall now. And he'd preferred it to the original.

They'd spent their nights listening to both versions, debating the pros and cons of each, he pointing out a guitar riff here, a key change there, while she applauded the purity of Roberta's vocals. They'd sing along and he'd grab his guitar. 'Listen,' he'd say, 'this is what I mean'. And she'd grin and nod and tell him it was great, but that she still favoured the original. Often their disputes went on into the early hours until, too tired to argue any more, they'd call a truce, fall into one another's arms and agree to disagree.

The fights were harmless at that stage of their relationship: light-hearted spats that ended in laughter and blissful making-up. And the song became *their* song.

Killing me...

She felt Teresa's fingernails digging into her arm.

'Hush, Mum.'

...softly

Maureen hadn't realised she'd been humming the tune aloud. She glanced around. All eyes were on her now. What were these people thinking? Did they suspect anything? She couldn't be sure.

'... in the sure and certain hope ...'

The vicar's mouth moved slowly and deliberately over each syllable as if savouring their taste.

'...the resurrection to eternal life.'

Maureen thought it a sensual mouth and wondered what it would be like to kiss.

Killing me...

Were vicars good kissers? She glanced sideways at Teresa, fearing she'd spoken the thought out loud. But this time the girl's eyes held no reproach, and her fingers rested easy in the crook of her mother's arm.

...softly

Steve was a good kisser. Had been. In the early days. Before...

The crows began to bicker. Beaks and talons clashed as they skittered upwards in a frenzy of flapping wings.

Killing me...

But it was soon over. The birds eyed one another for a moment and then settled down to continue their grisly activity.

Maureen shivered.

An easterly wind had struck up, sweeping across the graveyard and snatching at funeral garb, until coats and scarves began to flutter like crow feathers.

...softly

She had refused to wear black. Even though she knew it suited her. Steve had liked her in black; liked her skirts short, her tops tight; liked her hair upswept, her make-up pale, eyeliner dark and dramatic. But she'd chosen a different look today, picked out a softer shade for her outfit - presented a different version of herself. No crow-black widows' weeds for her, but grey, light as a pearl, with just a hint of periwinkle. *Dove,* the shop assistant had called it. That sold it for Maureen. *Dove:* the symbol of peace.

The vicar had stopped speaking. Teresa was scooping up a handful of soil.

Maureen stooped and followed suit. The sticky mass tumbled from her fingers and landed in a solid thump on the coffin's brass plate, obliterating part of the wording. But everyone knew what it said: 'Stephen John Stone,' it said. 'R.I.P'.

Tragic.

They all thought so. Said as much.

A life cut short.

All true. But what about *her* life?

What about me? she wanted to yell. What about what he did to me?

Killing me...

But he couldn't touch her now. Not now. Thank God.

'Merciful God...' The vicar was winding up.

Maureen heard a sob. She looked around. Dry eyes stared back. Teresa's grip tightened. 'Hush, Mum.'

'Amen,' the vicar said.

...softly

It began to rain, fine weeping drizzle, bringing with it a swirling mist and a drop in temperature. Having paid their last respects, the shivering mourners shuffled backwards and started to drift away. Maureen watched them go, heads down, collars up. A few umbrellas bloomed, the movements disturbing the birds again. Up they flew, crying out their protest as they soared. 'Haw-haw. Haw-haw.'

Maureen hated that crow call. It sounded like laughter, the cruel and mocking kind.

Steve had laughed that first time she'd had too much to drink. Not mocking. Not then. She'd been out with some workmates. They'd gone to hear a new band on the scene. Steve was the lead guitarist. There'd been a party afterwards, but Maureen wasn't used to alcohol. Steve had called her a lightweight and taken her home. He'd quite a following in those days; could have had his pick. That night, he picked her.

Killing me...

Reverend Timmins took her hand.

'God bless you, Maureen,' he murmured,

...softly

Maureen looked at the hand holding hers. She'd be willing to bet it had never once been raised in anger. She held on, wanting to keep him there, needing to say something. She opened her mouth to speak, searching for the right words, saw the vicar's expression change, and knew he'd smelt the whisky on her.

Killing me...

Maureen let go his hand. 'Thank you,' she said.

...softly

And left it at that.

The drinking had been fun at first; gave her a warm, floating feeling; broke down her inhibitions; let her be who she wanted to be; who Steve wanted her to be. But as time went by, things changed. *She* changed. And so did he. The drink made her weak; made *him* brutal.

Teresa clung to her mother's arm, leading her away. The funeral cars were beginning to leave.

She'd threatened to leave. After that first time.

Killing me...

But he begged her to stay. 'It won't happen again, babe,' he said.

...softly

'I swear it won't happen again.'

And it didn't. Not for months. And when it did, it was her fault. She'd antagonised him, he said. She always antagonised him.

Maureen watched the cars out of sight until only one remained. A few more steps and she'd made it.

There'd be no wake afterwards. No one to drink to his memory. None to keep her company while they chewed the fat and harked back to better times. There wasn't a soul to commiserate and regret her loss. Only Teresa. And she was just a kid.

Maureen slipped her arm around her daughter. 'You ok, love?' Teresa's face, so like her father's in profile, betrayed no emotion. But Maureen worried about the girl; about how she would cope with what had happened. She was at an impressionable age. It was bound to leave scars.

Teresa had been the cause of that last row. Steve was playing a local gig and she and the girl had tagged along for the ride. There'd been a new drummer in the band. Young. Not bad looking if you ignored the acne and the piercings. Teresa had taken a shine to him. She was growing up. They'd got talking during the break. No harm in it. Just a couple of kids having a laugh. But Steve didn't like it. 'Keep an eye on her,' he'd ordered.

She ought to have seen the warning signs: the mean set of his mouth, the contempt in his eyes. *What kind of a mother…?* Trouble was, she never learnt. And she laughed. Told him to relax and have another drink. Antagonising, see?

'Come on, Mum,' Teresa said. 'Let's go home,'

Steve didn't come home. Not that night. It was late morning before he showed and the drink was still on him.

'Bitch,' he yelled, and more besides.

The neighbours heard it; said so at the inquest. They'd heard the screams too.

Killing me...killing me...killing me...

And the silence.

...softly

Self-defence. That's what everyone assumed. Even the coroner. Well, there was no denying the injuries, was there?

'Bitch,' he'd yelled as he struck out. 'Bitch,' as his fist found its target, breaking her nose, and sending her sprawling.

And, one minute he'd been towering high above her, looking down on where she'd fallen, the next he was lying beside her, his lifeblood staining her floorboards.

And there, gazing down on them both, Teresa, the bone-handled kitchen knife still in her hand.

Killing me...

...softly

They'd got it wrong, those people. The chain of events was not as it seemed.

Same story...different version. But Maureen didn't mind. In fact, she preferred it to the original.

There was no sign of the crows as the last two mourners passed through the lych-gate and out into the circling mist. The funeral car was waiting. The driver held the door open and they both got in. It was over. They were going home.

Maureen sucked in a lungful of air. She closed her eyes, leant back on the seat's cushioned headrest, and gave herself up to the enveloping warmth of the car's interior. She breathed again; more easily this time, and began to relax as she listened to the rain drumming a steady rhythm on the roof overhead.

The tempo changed.

A fragment of melody crept into her head.

Killing me...

She began to hum.

...softly.

THIRD PLACE

Starlings

Norma Allen

Even though he shivered in the cold wind blowing along the front, the child would not move from the seat. The whipped up waves were sending cascades of water onto the prom, dark clouds were gathering and people hurried away.

'Let's go home for supper now. Nan will be waiting. It's your favourite.' Evan held his hand out to the child.

'No. Rhys stay. Birds.' He shrugged away from his grandfather and pointed up.

'They're starlings, Rhys, getting ready to rest for the night.' The child did not turn his head or speak.

The starlings were gathering in the dusk: rising and falling, weaving and turning, forming spirals in the air. More and more birds came and joined in the dance until it seemed the whole of the sky was full of their ever-changing synchronised movement.

The child remained silent, mesmerised, unaware of anything else around him. They'd stayed there until the last of the birds had dropped and settled under the pier. Only then did the boy allow Evan to take his hand and lead him home.

Sarah was peering out of the front window as they came up the path.

'There you are, at last. What were you thinking, keeping the child out in this cold wind? He'll catch his death.'

'Sorry, love. We were watching the murmuration. He wouldn't come away.'

Supper was on the table but the child pushed it aside. He fetched paper and began to draw. Sarah sighed and put the food to keep warm. They didn't want to have to deal with one of Rhys's tantrums.

It was perhaps half an hour before the child put down his pen and looked up. He did not show them the drawing but pushed it to one side.

Evan picked up the paper and saw with some surprise that the meticulous, seemingly random tiny marks the child had made with a black biro, revealed themselves as a sky full of swirling and looping birds.

'Why Rhys, this is wonderful.' He showed the drawing to Sarah. 'See, love it's the starlings.'

She nodded, adjusting her glasses to look more closely. 'The boy's got talent, he really has.'

She bent down to Rhys. 'Clever boy, you've drawn the starlings.'

Rhys ignored her and carried on wolfing down his food.

All these years later Evan still had that first drawing displayed in the little box- room where Rhys had slept when he stayed.

That had been the first time. The child would agitate to go and see the starlings every evening he was with them. Not that he called them starlings. Try as they might they could not get Rhys to say that word. It was always, *Birds. See birds!*

He took him up to the prom at dusk whenever he could. Rhys always came back to draw what he'd seen. It kept him occupied for hours. Of course, as spring came the display ceased. The birds had flown off for the summer. The boy had not understood. He was often angry. At the time he and Sarah had realised that their grandchild was somehow *different*. Their daughter, Bethan, had been defensive.

'He's just late talking, that's all, Mam. Bryn says he'll soon catch up.'

He didn't though and eventually the diagnosis came. Rhys was autistic. He'd need extra care all his life. At first Bethan would not accept it.

'I'm not having that. Those doctors can be wrong. I know my own child. He just wants extra attention and I'll give it to him. He'll be fine, you'll see.'

When he wasn't, she became convinced it was all her fault.

'I should never have drunk wine in the early months. I can't imagine why I did.'

'But you didn't even know you were pregnant then, love.' Sarah would try to soothe her. 'I'm sure it's nothing to do with that.'

'What is it to do with then, Mam? It must have been because I didn't bond with him at first. Yes, that's it.'

Bryn, Bethan's husband, struggled with the knowledge that his boy would never be the son he wanted. Inevitably, their relationship suffered. Things became worse between them as the child's demands and challenging behaviour grew.

'We can't look after him properly, Beth. Rhys will have to go into a home. He'll be better off there and we can get on with our lives. Maybe have another child.'

'Our Rhys is not going into any home. How can you even think such a thing, Bryn? We'll manage.'

In the end Bryn had left and they had eventually divorced. Although he paid maintenance for the child, he did not want to have any more to do with his son and soon moved away from the area.

They had supported their daughter as much as they could. Rhys was often difficult but he was their kin and they loved him. They would have him to stay to give her a break now and then. But the child's frustrations grew and as he became older and stronger he became more unmanageable. Eventually, he'd been found a place in a special school. It was nearly an hour's drive away but the child was picked up and dropped off each day by minibus. They'd been assured that this would be the best way to help Rhys and it was. He was calmer, spoke a little more and was happy enough if he had a pencil in his hand.

This evening, Evan, passing down the prom on his way to the club, saw that the murmuration had begun. It was cold but clear and dry, the setting sun a golden backdrop to the display. Many others had come to see the sight, wondering at the ability of the birds never to collide. Scientists would be able to explain it but, to most people, it was as if they had some mysterious signalling system. Evan had seen it many times but he couldn't resist sitting on the seat to watch. That's what had brought it all back to him, of course.

When the boy was getting towards secondary age he'd been offered a place for the following year in an excellent residential school for youngsters on the autistic spectrum on the outskirts of London. There, his needs would be met and his talent for drawing nurtured. Bethan was distraught at first.

'It's so far away. I'll hardly ever see him. I can't let him go.'

Sarah, ever the practical one, had said: 'Maybe, when the time comes, you could move over there to be near him; sell your house here and rent a flat perhaps. You'd easily get secretarial work. Not that we want you to go love, but it seems it's the best way for Rhys.'

'I agree,' Evan had said, even though he hated the thought of their only child leaving. 'We need to think of the boy. It's a wonderful opportunity for him. And it's not the other end of the earth, we can visit and keep in touch.'

That had been the plan for a few months until Sarah became ill.

'You're looking tired love,' he said one day, noticing how pale and thin she was.

'I'm fine, don't fuss.'

'Why not have a check up with the doc? Can't do any harm.'

Reluctantly, she'd agreed. The night before the appointment she told him she'd found a lump in her breast a few months before.

'I didn't want to worry you and there's been a lot of more important things to think about with Rhys and Bethan. It'll just be a cyst, you'll see.'

It wasn't a cyst but cancer and by then at an advanced stage. There was nothing to be done except keep Sarah comfortable for whatever time she had left.

Bethan sold her house and moved in with them. It had been difficult with Rhys but he'd provided some distraction from the pain the family were in.

They hadn't said much to Rhys except that Nan was ill. When he came home from school he'd go up to her bedroom and sit by the bed doing his drawings.

Sarah had slipped away early one morning within a few months of her diagnosis. Her body had been moved while the boy was at school. They had tried to explain to the child but he hadn't understood. It had been distressing to see him searching for her in all the rooms in the house, looking under the beds and in the cupboards and wardrobes.

'Where Nan, Granfer? Where Nan?' he kept shouting.

Evan had struggled with the loss of his beloved Sarah. They'd been together since they were teenagers. He'd dreaded the time when Bethan and the boy would be gone too.

'I won't leave you, Dad, not now,' she'd said, 'Rhys can go to his new school. I'll just have to travel to see him when I can.'

'No, Beth, I won't let you do that. You need to be near your son. I'll come up and visit you sometimes, stay in a hotel or something if your flat isn't big enough.' Eventually, she'd agreed.

At first, Evan had found it hard to come home from work each night to an empty house. He'd often stop at the pub, meaning only to stay for one then find himself staggering home at closing time. He'd wander around the rooms, searching – much like the child had done, even talking to Sarah at times.

Bethan kept in touch, telephoning most days, telling him how well Rhys was doing and how she'd found a good job. She came home some weekends and he even went to stay with her. Once, she'd taken him to visit Rhys at his school. It was a well-run place and the youngsters looked happy but his grandson, now a tall young lad, didn't seem to recognise him at all.

'It's because he's not expecting to see you here, Dad. When I get a chance we'll come to Wales, I'm sure once he sees your home, he'll remember.' All the same it had hurt.

She'd never brought him though. Her visits became further apart as did the phone calls. *I've got to let her live her own life*, he thought and I must get on with mine.

Friends and neighbours were good to him and eventually, even after he'd retired, he found a way of filling his days. He had his garden to tend, walks by the sea, evenings playing dominoes or darts down the club and each year on his birthday a visit from Bethan.

She had phoned last night.

'Sorry, I haven't been in touch for a while Dad. Just rang to wish you a happy seventieth birthday for tomorrow. Are you doing anything special?'

'It'll be a quiet one as usual, I expect. How is Rhys? Is he still working in that art gallery?'

'He's doing well and selling a lot of his work.'

'That's good. Any chance of you coming down for a visit? You know your and Rhys's rooms are always ready.' At one time she never failed to come for his birthday.

'We're so busy, Dad. We'll manage it one of these days. Do you still go up the prom to watch the starlings?'

No visit this year then. Well, he was too old to make a fuss about his birthday. He'd arranged to see a couple of mates down the club. He'd go on down once he'd watched the birds for a bit.

He didn't notice them until they were close, until Rhys had sat down beside him on the seat and the young man had tugged at his sleeve.

'Look, Granfer - starlings!'

2020 YOUNG WRITERS' SHORT STORY AWARD WINNER

Young Writers' Short Story Award Judge's Report

Stephen Bywater

I was honoured to be asked to be one of the judges for The Bedford Competition and I thoroughly enjoyed reading the shortlist of entries for the Young Writers' Short Story Award. Congratulations goes to Kirsten Udall for winning the competition. Her short story, entitled *Black Bin Bags,* was a tremendous piece of writing: strong narrative voice, quite dark, quite manic. It certainly drew me in and I have no doubt that it will transport any reader. The other stories were also very strong indeed and had it been a different judge, it might well have been a different outcome.

Black Bin Bags

Kirsten Udall

The food in this house spoils too quickly. Milk lasts a couple of days, cheese goes black after a week and we have six rotten eggs rotting away on the top shelf of our fridge. *He* never took enough care to shut the damned thing properly and nothing can keep if the conditions are wrong. The conditions are wrong for everything here. It all expires before it should.

We have no black bin bags left either. It's always been *his* job to get those. We only have the see-through ones we use for recycling and I can't use them to throw away the spoiled food. Marilyn's curtains would twitch gleefully if I did that. No – I won't do it. She's not allowed that satisfaction. The kitchen will simply have to smell rancid for another day until *he* brings some home. No doubt, *he* will moan about the smell when *he* walks through the door but I also have no doubt that *he* will do nothing about it. Spite will drive me to dwell in this sewer until my skin turns black. I'm fine with that. *He* has to buy the bin bags.

I shut the windows, denying the house fresh air. Now the smell is contained, it intensifies. I gag. I smile. *He* will hate it. But that still isn't enough. It's bad but not bad enough to force *him* to buy them. I shut the curtains too. The house is choked by darkness and I am nesting in its foul throat. I bring my hands up to my own and swallow, feeling the bile fall and rise up again inside. I want him to know this. I want him to live this. I want to see him vomiting so violently that his vital organs pool at his feet. I want his skin to scale over when he tries to scuttle away from the smell. I want to see his body convulse as he falls to the floor and chokes on his own tongue. I want to bear witness to it all. And then I want to tell people that he died because he forgot to bring home black bin bags. A cautionary tale to the domesticated man.

The phone is ringing now. I wouldn't usually answer, but it's rung twice already and takes too long to go to voicemail. I pick up the phone. It's *his* mother. The crow who raised an incompetent son.

'Sylvie – are you there?' she squawks.

I answer, 'yes'.

'Oh, my dear. How *are* you?'

I answer, 'fine'. I ask her the same.

'Well – you know…'

I do know.

'Have I caught you at a bad time?'

She has.

'I'll ring you back later.'

I don't really care whether she does or whether she doesn't. I won't be picking up either way.

I turn back to the food in the fridge now. The fridge light is dim from the time it has spent exhausting itself trying to preserve what's left of the good inside. I don't blame it for giving up. It can only do so much with the door left open. A swamp of raw meat juice is festering at the bottom and I realise that I'm disappointed: no maggots. I don't know how to make them come, though, and I won't turn my mobile on to google it. It hasn't been switched on for weeks and I don't have the stomach for it now. I am too busy digesting other things.

I'm slowly getting used to the smell now but that's not what I want. So, even though it's midday in mid-June, I turn the heating on and wait. *He* would kill me for wasting *his* money but, to my delight, the revulsion returns. I turn the oven on next and I am devoured again by disgust. I heave in a most heavenly way as the thickness of the air engulfs me. Sheer divinity suffocates me with spoiled meat and methane. Around me, greasy hot tentacles begin to unfurl themselves. They seize the tip of my nose. Then, they trail slime up my nostrils. They're creeping further and further and further. It hurts. I can feel them digging for my organs, rooted behind my eyes. I know they're reaching for my lungs further and further and further still. I can't breathe. I don't want to breathe. *He* will find me blue on the ground.

But then, a slam of the letterbox. They retract.

My body betrays me by breathing again. Eyes adjusted to the darkness, I stagger through the stench towards the front door where I see a perfect pale envelope taunting me from the ground. I scream. My release – my surrender – now just another thing in this house spoiled too soon. I spit on the envelope as I did with every one that had come before. *He* would be mad at me for that. It could be from *his* Uncle Ernest or *his* cousin, Kurt, or *his* ex-girlfriend, Evelyn, or someone else that had never concerned themselves with me before. Yes, it'll be addressed to me but written for *him. He* doesn't deserve that.

I wade barefoot back towards the twisted comfort of the dirty kitchen. I feel the veil of dead flowers draped beneath me on the floor. I had gotten sick of watching so many of them wilt a week ago, but I couldn't throw them away. Not out of sentiment or anything – I had no black bin bags. Instead, I had to watch them die on the laminate. At least with the curtains closed, I don't have to look at them anymore. I never want to smell the sweetness of flowers again. At my funeral, I want every flower in sight drowned in vinegar. It's much more fitting for the occasion. I want my body left unburied too. I want it to be a symbol of premature expiry – the kind that cursed my house. Then leave my decomposing corpse to pollute the air with odours so offensive even the vultures vomit around me. Then, make *him* clean it up.

Because *he* started it all. *He* is the reason for the spit-drenched cards at our door. *He* is the one who caused this stench. *He* bought the milk. *He* bought the cheese. *He* bought the eggs. *He* never shut the fridge door properly. *He* bought the faulty thing to begin with. *He* would hate the smell. *He* would moan about the smell. *He* would buy the bin bags because of the smell. But *he* forgot the black bin bags that day and *he* isn't coming back to buy us more.

2020 BEDFORD SHORT STORY PRIZE WINNER

Bedford Short Story Prize Judge's Report

Neil Beardmore

It was a pleasure and privilege to judge the Bedford short story prize. I was impressed by how unique and enjoyable the stories were. They were all ambitious in themes but very confidently written. Dealing with relationships, character and everyday issues in compassionate sincere ways without any sentimentalizing.

Every story I read was serious and dedicated, and I could see that the writers were very keen to get their work across. They are all well researched and very authentic. I am still excited about how a local area can produce such a diversity of themes, and all competently crafted and written, well done to everyone. I looked at and rated each story according to character, captivation, credibility, atmosphere, beginning, ending, struggle, point of view, narrative and other things, and I can say that I got something from each one. As far as I'm concerned, we have a winner, but many runners up, and they all have the talent to develop. Like all things, if you keep doing it, you get better, you develop your voice and you mature in style.

The story I chose as the winner, *Barates and My Father*, is a story that explores, from the children's point of view, relationships, grief, the trials of fitting in, and forced relocation to another culture. It is about tender relationships, about empathy, about how we touch each other emotionally. A lot to get into a short story, but it is very effective, and is written without any sentimentality or melodrama. This story is very well crafted and very well researched. I particularly enjoyed the dialogue, expressing the meeting of two different struggling cultures. There is also a fascinating historical backstory, which really adds to it. I was truly moved and impressed.

Barates and My Father

Fran Maciver

It was the brooch, in the shape of a horse and rider, that first drew him to that part of the museum. Emir thought it was funny and beautiful at the same time. A little man with an overlarge head and tiny feet astride his steed. Emir hadn't intended to go to *Arbeia*, but he'd missed his bus and had time to kill. His sister had told him about the Roman fort and museum she'd visited with her Year 3 class, so he'd walked the fifteen minutes there from the bus station. His friend, Addie, had also visited and Emir was curious.

The brooch brought sad memories. His mother, Amira, now dead, had once owned a few treasured pieces of jewellery, in what she had called *the blessed times* in Syria. Emir could vaguely recall a silver brooch of a prancing horse and two beaten silver rings, intertwined and bound together in the shape of a vine, lying in a basket in his mother's bedroom. That, of course, was before the civil war, before all the bombs and sniper bullets and incendiaries had rained down on his home. Before death danced to its own beat on the streets. Now lost. All lost.

At fifteen, Emir, tall for his age and on the brink of manhood, would've expected to have been taken into his father's business. Fahad had been a respected baker in a small town, two miles north of Homs. *Had been* being very much the key words. The long, drawn-out civil war, beginning with pro-democracy demonstrations in Deraa in 2011, was a conflict that had surrounded Emir and his sister, Khadijar, aged eight, most of their lives, for the whole of hers. It had changed everything. Future dreams had exploded in the hell that was his home country, a peaceful, seemingly tameable uprising turned into a raging beast of a vicious, multi-sided, civil war.

Now, his father was dead, killed by a sniper's bullet, six months before Emir and his sister came to the UK under the *Syrian Vulnerable Persons Resettlement Scheme*, (SVPRS). Fahad and Khadijar had been out fetching water from the only remaining source in their rubble-strewn neighbourhood. Only Khadijar returned. Emir could remember his father with his arm around him, sitting in the remains of their home two days before his death, urging his son: 'Be a leader with integrity, Emir. Your name means just that, so don't always be a follower. Look after your mother when I'm not there.' *When,* not *if.* He seemed to know.

Prophetic words.

Emir bent down slowly, better to see the little man on the horse in the museum display. Standing up and stretching his shoulders, he ran long, fine-boned fingers through the black tangle of curly hair, trying to push back defiant tendrils from a high, olive-skinned forehead. His was not yet a handsome face, in the conventional sense of the word, but it was an interesting face – expressive, even in his teens – dark eyes, long lashes, the fuzz of a beard, a straight nose and wide mouth.

When he rode on public transport, Emir did his best to avoid eye contact, preferring to look straight ahead, feigning indifference about any stares, those from girls especially. Being a refugee meant there was always the need to blend in. He'd already suffered a few taunts of *terrorist* at school when teachers weren't around to hear.

In these last two years, he'd tried so hard to fit in, particularly on arrival, when he didn't feel he belonged to any place, when fear had sat on his shoulder for so long. He wanted to shout aloud about losing everything. Though most were supportive and thoughtful, some people in Tarrant Bay, South Shields, tended to act as if, for the Syrian refugees accepted in the town and its neighbourhood, *one size fitted all*. They meant well. They couldn't know about the flashbacks he still suffered, or his waking many nights to hear Khadijar crying softly in the bedroom she shared with Steph. When her father had died, she was so badly shocked that she spoke little for some time afterwards. On arrival in the UK, if anyone asked her questions about Syria, she would fall silent and tears filled her eyes.

Emir and his sister lived with Mr and Mrs Graham, foster carers, and Steph, their *surprise*, last-born, aged seven. A *canny bairn*, her mum called her. Older, working brother, Sam, lived in a flat above a corner chippie on the seafront. 'Convenient', the neighbours commented, and they were right.

'You'll soon get used to the way of things around here, pet,' encouraged neighbour, Mrs Foley, as Emir helped her wash some windows at the front of her terraced house, next door but one. 'Them's capable hands. I'm a good judge of hands.' She stepped back, breathing heavily, her face red and sweaty and adjusted the floral apron around her stout figure. 'Them top windows was right clouty. Howay, pet. Time for a brew.'

Emir had to adapt quickly to survive, to fit in. Nevertheless, he strove to show he'd got his own abilities and preferences. In a way, it was like being *born again*. He'd made one friend early on. Adrian - *Addie* to his mates at Emir's school, in Year 11. One Saturday, he'd noticed and recognised Emir and his sister watching him from behind the goal. Addie lived on the same terraced street. He, too, being dyslexic and with a startling shock of red hair that made him stand out, hadn't, in his early years, had an easy time fitting in at school.

'Seen you before,' said Addie at the match, stuffing an orange piece into his mouth at half-time, 'you was helping Mrs Foley with them windows. I'm Addie – live next door but one, up the street from you. Oh, aye, you live with Mr and Mrs Graham and Steph, don't you?'

Khadijar had remained silent, resolutely looking down.

Emir's English was better than his sister's, so he'd been able to cement the friendship. He'd picked up bits and pieces of English from Abbas, father of two in the next-door tent, in the Lebanese refugee camp just over the Syrian border. Abbas had worked in a bank, before it was hit by an incendiary, killing most of the staff.

'Teaching you, Emir, helps me forget the things I've seen – the army tanks, the blood and death everywhere. I feel useful here, not just a number, a nobody – a 'refugee'. Now, come on, tell me how to say in English, 'my name is …?'

Addie was bold enough to ask Emir the occasional question about Syria, where others, especially adults, were afraid to intrude. Emir coped with that from his school friend, whereas, with others, he clammed up. The older lad tried not to crowd Emir at school or be too protective, preferring to quietly watch out for him.

Hetty Graham, a buxom, enthusiastic Tyne-sider – no wilting violet – was married to Mick, a jobbing painter and decorator working in Sunderland. Her florid face, framed by greying hair scraped back into a bun at the nape of her neck, reflected her warm nature. Her end-of-terrace house was an open one - welcoming. Hetty often invited Addie back for casserole meals after school, when his single-parent mum had a shift at the local pub. Sometimes, the two school mates went down to the local chip-shop to give Hetty a break and dropped in on Sam to talk *serious stuff* – football. But last night, it'd been lamb cobbler on the menu at home.

'We've known it hard, Emir. Oh, aye, pet.' She stretched out her hand to Addie across the table in the kitchen. 'Ee, give us your plate.' Mrs Graham plonked two large spoons of lamb stew and potato in front of him. 'My grand-da worked in John Readhead and Sons, shipbuilders until the gates shut for good in '84. My Mick was made jobless in '93 when the colliery closed and our firstborn, Sam, was only a toddler of three years. Oh aye, our family's known hardship, too, Emir. You don't get nowt for sittin' on yer hands. We would'na made it through if my Mick hadn't turned to decoratin'. Sam's joined him in business. He's a canny lad and no mistake – got a contract for him and his da' – local housing estate's going up. I was owa the moon when they got taken on by Geesons.' Turning to Emir, 'More hotpot, pet?'

In the museum, feeling suddenly tired and dispirited after seeing the horseman brooch, Emir wandered over to a chair in the corner of the next room, laid his rucksack on the wood floor and sat down. No one else seemed to be around. He stared blankly across at some Roman pottery, letting his mind drift. He wasn't certain if the Grahams really knew what a hard life was. How could they know what it was really like to be so close to death for so long?

Naturally, Emir missed his parents; his father he missed greatly. Sometimes it hurt so bad even to think of him – like an animal in his gut, gnawing away. Then, in the Lebanese refugee camp, Emir's mother, Amira, had died of pneumonia. Winters there were bitter, and they were living in tents. She was already frail, with a chest infection, when they arrived at the camp before the Aid agencies and doctors got involved. Once Amira knew her children were safe, it seemed like she gave up. The children nearly gave up too, but Emir remembered his father's words – 'be a leader, Emir'. Somehow, they'd got through it and survived.

Emir took a packet of chewing-gum from the side pocket of the rucksack, a present from *Mrs G*, as he'd learnt to call her when he first went off to his secondary school. He popped the packet in his pocket and sat there chewing, remembering the shock of being given gifts at Christmas and Eid – new school textbooks, a football jersey and even a phone.

'A'way, pet. Ya canna gan t'school with no bag for ya books,' she'd said, as he opened a huge Christmas-wrapped parcel and looked at the contents.

Mick and Hetty also gave Khadijar a new pair of jeans, a sparkly top and a matching hijab.

'Ee, Khadijar,' cried Mick, after she'd opened her gift, 'you'll look a reet bobby dazzla in that outfit. Won't she, hinny?' Mrs G smiled proudly, agreeing.

Emir remembered that in the camp in Lebanon he'd been given teddy bears when he'd wanted so much to have books and another blanket to keep out the cold.

A middle-aged woman clutching several clipboards entered the gallery. She smiled across at Emir and he remembered seeing her at school when she gave a talk to the Year 10s about *The Roman Army and South Shields*. Much to his surprise, she came across to him.

'I'm sorry, pet. We're closing in another twenty minutes. George'll be along with his keys soon.' She was about to turn away but changed her mind. 'Haven't I met you at The Robert McAlister School?'

Emir looked up into a smiling face. Shoulder-length, fair hair, curled inwards on her neck. Pointed chin with a cleft in it. Snub nose and laughter lines at the corners of two ice-blue eyes. A slight, slender figure, reminding him of his mum.

He took the chewing-gum from his mouth and dropped it in a nearby bin.

'Yes. You came and give history talk.'

'So, I did, pet. You were the one asked about Hadrian's Wall, weren't you?'

He nodded, pleased she'd remembered.

'Excuse me for asking, but are you bilingual?'

'Yes, I'm Syrian. I speak,' here, he thought for a moment, 'three languages – four.'

She smiled.

He went on – 'Arabic; a dialect like Arabic – my mother's language; English and' – his turn to smile – 'and a bit of, how you say – Geordie.'

She laughed at this point, understanding his humour. 'I came from Birmingham, so I, also, had to learn fast.'

'I too.'

'You may not remember my name. I'm Pat Stephenson. I work here.'

Emir introduced himself.

Suddenly, as if making up her mind, she asked, 'Have you seen this over here?' She walked to a display nearby. He followed.

The upright stone slab, found at the Roman fort, Arbeia, showed a woman, bracelets on her wrists, seated on a tall-backed chair, opening a treasure-box on her right-hand side, with what looked to Emir to be a basket of wool on the other. There was some writing below. Why was Mrs Stephenson so keen to show it to him?

Pointing at the words cut into the sandstone, she explained: 'This is a tombstone set up to the memory of a freed, British woman called *Regina, queen*, by her husband – 'from the *Catuvellauni*' – a tribe living in the south – married to a man from Palmyra called *Barates*; thirty years old when she died…'

Emir interrupted her. 'If she was *freedwoman*, does that mean she was – what's the word – um, a…?'

'A *slave* – got it, Emir. Most likely, she was originally his household slave. Can you see something under the Roman lettering at the bottom?'

'Yes, I can. It looks a bit like my language – Arabic.'

'It's actually Aramaic, so no wonder you thought it was familiar. Clever of you, Emir. It says, *Regina, freedwoman of Barates. Alas*.'

'What is *alas*?'

Mrs Stephenson explained. Emir thought for a moment.

'Barates, he loved his wife, *Regina*, much to put such things, and – he pointed to the stone – make this for her.'

'I'm sure he did. He was far from home, but he clearly loved his *queen* – his wife.'

Suddenly, he felt swamped in a tide of sadness, *empathy* his English teacher would've called it if Emir had understood the English. Why did he feel sad looking at this old tombstone? He was thinking about his parents. Emir didn't want Mrs Stephenson to see his reaction, so he quickly asked another question.

'Was Barates Roman soldier at the fort?'

'We don't think so; soldiers weren't allowed to have wives and there's no mention after his name of an army unit. See here.' She pointed to the lettering. 'He might have been a trader to the fort, selling goods to the military.

'Where's Palmyra? Is it in Italy?'

'Oh my, no. It's in Syria! It was an ancient city in the present region of Homs; part of what was once a huge empire stretching over several countries, including Syria.'

Emir looked down at the floor, suddenly quiet.

'Have I said something upsetting, Emir?' she asked, full of concern.

He turned back to the tombstone. More silent seconds, then – 'we lived in a village near Homs. It's gone now.' His voice wavered. 'It's all gone.' Now he was blinking back tears.

'Oh, Emir, you must think me so insensitive. I remember now – I remember the *Shields Comet*, a few years back, coming out with an article on the Syrian refugee resettlement scheme, the SVPRS I think it's shortened to. Were you part of that?'

He still didn't turn round to her but kept his eyes fixed resolutely on the tombstone. A few more seconds passed. 'My father died in village,' he spoke, falteringly, 'my mother later in Lebanon. She died in camp.' Now he turned back to her. 'Yes, I'm part of that thing you said. I'm Syrian, but I don't want to be called *refugee* anymore.

'No, of course not.' There was mutual silence for a while. Emir crossed the room to retrieve his rucksack, but he didn't walk away out to the Entrance. He went back to Regina's tombstone.

Pat was still by the display, looking at Barates and his *queen*, seated, in homely fashion, on her wicker chair, looking out at them across the centuries. This time, Emir smiled. He, also, stared again at the long-dead wife of the Syrian and spoke, without looking at Mrs Stephenson next to him:

'That Barates, he was good man to do that for his wife, wasn't he, Mrs Stephenson?'

'Yes, Emir. He was.'

'He made it, made the journey *here*, like my sister and me. All the way from Homs to the UK.'

'Yes. All the way to Roman-ruled *Britannia*, to this fortress of Arbeia.'

Emir shouldered his rucksack. 'My father – his name's Fahad – he'd like to see this. Make him feel good. You understand?'

Mrs Stephenson nodded. 'I do indeed.' She smiled again, such a warm smile. 'I must go now and check the other gallery.'

When she'd gone, Emir took one last look. Somehow, he was sure Barates would've understood how he felt – this UK, it was his home now, yet he wasn't completely one with this new country. Maybe soon it would be different. Until then, he had Barates and Regina as *friends* he could visit.

He imagined Barates and Regina would've had children. He imagined Barates bustling about in this fort of Arbeia, watching over his cartloads of cloth and other goods. He saw him bargaining with the officers for a good price, just like his mother had in the market in Homs, before the war dropped terror into the streets and villages everywhere. He imagined Barates and Regina hugging each other in the evening. Barates would have got on well with his father. *Barates* and *Fahad* – it sounded good. 'Barates and my father,' he murmured to himself. He was sure he and Khadijah would settle well in South Shields. But they'd not forget their home country and would pray for peace there.

'Yes, Barates – friend,' he said quietly to the empty room. Taking one last look at the merchant's regal wife on her chair, he popped another piece of chewing-gum in his mouth, turned on his heel and left the gallery.

2020 POETRY COMPETITION

Poetry Competition Judge's Report

Lesley Saunders

I would like to salute all the entrants who sent in their poems to the competition – I know from experience that it takes courage to submit one's work for scrutiny and judgement by someone else. By entering the competition all the writers have taken themselves and their writing just a bit more seriously; my advice to people who weren't successful in this competition is, keep trying but above all keep writing!

I decided to read all the entries, because, as one of the organisers said, 'each poem means something to someone and many of them reflect the frustration and loneliness that all the restrictions have brought about'. I felt that reading every poem would be an appropriate way to honour the depth of emotion that people have experienced in this extraordinarily difficult and sad year. I encountered many poems whose great pathos, anguish even, was testament to how we look to poetry to hold and express our deepest feelings.

Unsurprisingly, several common themes emerged among the poems: the pandemic and its effects, of course; the tragedy of war / poverty / disaster / neglect / destruction of the environment; the healing power of walking in nature / by the sea; the mystery of new life; experiences of mental distress / illness; the negative effects of modern technology; lost / regretted / unrequited love; the joy of sex; hate / revenge poetry; memories of misspent youth; a favourite animal / pet; what it is / was like to be someone else; advice for living; the passing of time; bereavement; and poems about writing a poem. Often, the poems that immediately grabbed my attention were those that started from somewhere quite different; although many poems that addressed one or other of those themes also made it on to my long-list.

Every judge has to work with some criteria, whether implicitly or explicitly. Mine usually include such writerly aspects as:

- originality and imaginative power
- ability to attract and sustain readers' interest
- strength of communication
- technical quality (including grammar, spelling, punctuation, formal and stylistic control).

At the outset I was looking for the poems that – because of their flair and deftness in handling their chosen subject – could take me by surprise, perhaps even make me wish I'd written them. To get to a manageable long-list, the process then became a more negative one, of finding reasons not to include a particular poem. I set aside poems whose forms took precedence over their themes, or whose lack of technical facility had not been able to fulfil their evident ambition of intention. In the last stage of long-listing, I had to discriminate between the 'near-misses' and the 'still-in-with-a-chance'.

The poems that I went on to short-list showed a strong engagement with their chosen subject-matter, which they interpreted in very different and original ways; I liked especially the ones that made unexpected connections. Secondly, they managed to sustain our interest – which may require different devices from those that capture our attention initially, including not giving everything away at once. It took me much thought and deliberation before I was able to pin down the prize-winning poems.

Third Prize goes to *Hymn* – a poem of surface simplicity with a deep emotional undertow, it conjures up a series of vivid enduring images including the surprising final line that is ambivalent about whether redemption or threat is being offered – which seems wholly truthful.

I awarded second place to *Passing and Meeting*, a prose poem full of intrigue, poignancy and desire, a condensed epic, a life journey through different modes of being, shape-shifting, fathomless and far-reaching, like a modern version of a folk-myth: magical!

The winning poem, *Toy Mouse, Discovered at Vindolanda Roman Fort, May 2020* , captivated me the first time I was reading through the entire pile of entries, and luckily I appreciated it more each time I read it. The evocation of other lives and times on the island of Britain is done with an economy of detail, and the ancient superstition to ward off plague is neatly laid without comment next to the modern archaeologist's 'wishful thinking' and the 'auguries' 'we dream up for ourselves'. The relationship between past and present is given contemporary nuance without being heavy-handed – the toy mouse is the perfect vehicle for this, as well as being a joy in itself.

WINNER

Toy Mouse, Discovered at Vindolanda Roman Fort, May 2020

Isabella Mead

A strip of leather, rodent-sized, with whiskers,
curved tail, ears, soft incisions for fur,
unearthed near a temple, hunched and attentive;

unexpected, like sunlight, and mischievous:
he chooses to make his reappearance
now, as the dark cities stir with fever;

a subversive reminder that Pliny the Elder
suggested kissing a mouse on the mouth
as an ideal cure. Or else it's no more

than the wishful thinking of an archaeologist
to sift through a thousand leather cuttings
and distinguish this: an atonement, a gift

from the god Apollo, the Lord of Mice,
who sent a plague on silver arrows
in a fit of anger; and now, as healer,

sending this, a playful semblance, a trace
of the real disease. A little vaccine.
As sunset falls behind Hadrian's Wall

we dream up auguries for ourselves
from secret hoards, fine-combing the earth
for the fortunes it holds. How Apollo was born

clutching a sword, and the cities turned gold.

SECOND PLACE

Passing and Meeting

Molly Underwood

We were sea-faring men, you and I. Another year, we might have been rivals—crossed each other, even—but the sea gave full and plenty, through that winter. We'd weathered worse. We learnt with leathered fingers, angled tightly, wanting water; fed each other fishflesh, wrung and writhing. You were wet, and I was shipwrecked nightly.

Love and death, tired titans! Each makes a horror of the other. We were kids that went to war for one another—wrote each other,

> *"Love, I would not leave you lightly"*
> *"You are a better muddied gun than I"*
> *"Tomorrow I die. Live. Love another boy. And keep my letters."*

We were women that rose together, steamed in the sun, to rub our linen raw before we bent big arms about each other, aching. I was run-off, running muddy from the scrubbing stone—I was fat and ashes, wrongly rendered—till some bit of bedding pulled us taut together; joined us, in its laying. Forehead to forehead, there we faced each other, frozen breath a folded ghost between us, and our tubs ran over. Some things stay the same. We stripped the sheets and, lines untied, undid each other tidy.

We learned early how to lose each other. Ballast-bellied, so it goes: we capsized slow, and drowned in shallow water—O, but we learned early how to love each other. I was drenched. Time spun me dry, and older, scaled and salted, smeared and tallowed, pointlessly I pitched to change the rudder:

> *"I dreamt I met you in the night & rode you home*
> *through German Bight & Humber."*

Like ships passing in the white sheets of Dover, we shuddered together, left each other wanting; wanting, found a way back to each other.

THIRD PLACE

Hymn

Harriet Sanders

Chapel by the sea, the salt-song leaves
crystals sharp along the edges of the stonework –
make your fingers bleed red stains for the sun
to shine through like glass.

Now that grass grows over the bronze
bell-song – listen – the gulls are calling prayers
wider, wilder, where the steeple used to stand
against the horizon. Chapel,

by the sea with a tilted altar and no roof,
there are wasps nesting in the pews.
Now in the middle of their hymn – if you
stay still – they light on you, humming.

Calling my mother

Anne Casey

I read somewhere there's a man in Japan who installed a telephone
to the dead at the end of his garden: for privacy reasons. it is inside
a white phone box with lines of tiny shiny glass panes like you might
see on any Tokyo street corner and a row of characters I can't make out
etched into the painted wooden trim around the top; by all appearances,
it has become quite popular—some ten thousand souls having made
the pilgrimage to the little garden on the outskirts of Otsuchi: you can
get there by high-speed train from Tokyo and you will find it just north
of Dai Chiwari 11; if you come to Dai Chiwari 12, you have gone too far—
a fact that frankly leaves me somewhat startled... much as I would love
to take the trip to Japan (due to my appalling sense of direction, almost
certainly relying on Google Maps if going all that way) to visit this man
and see his garden telephone box for making calls to the dead, enfolded
now in sleeping winter trees: a few buds will start to appear soon on the
stark cherry branches standing sentinel in the chill air carrying a trace of
salt from the Pacific just visible in the distance—much as I would truly
love to go whenever I want to talk to you, I just do... s*ometimes out loud*
if I'm in the car on my own, for instance, as to anyone standing next to me
at the lights, I might be on Bluetooth—that nice man in Japan should maybe
invent a mobile version for people who can't make it over to his lovely garden
where pink puffs will unfurl into sunlit air not too far from now (I wonder if
he might think of installing a little seat, maybe a wooden bench for people
waiting their turn to use the telephone to the dead)... *sometimes just in my head*
if the kids are home, for example, and I wouldn't want to spook them with
thoughts I've finally cracked or we have ghosts in the house again after all
we did to get rid of them that last time (Jack at eighteen months flapping
his chubby arms high above his head frantically and calling *Peoples....*
peoples going up...Up, up, up... in the sky!); we wouldn't have minded
so much if we had known one or two of them personally and they hadn't
made such a nuisance of themselves... *but mostly,* mostly, I have no need
for telephones or bluetooth, satellites or FaceTime or Snapchat, and even
though I can't make out your words any more, your answer comes through
loud and clear... *mostly* I have no need for that lovely shiny white telephone
box for talking to the dead at the end of the garden in sight of the Pacific
in the foothills of Otsuchi linked by train from Tokyo city because I just
talk to you by heart as I am quite sure that very kind-hearted man in Japan
would understand if ever we were to meet—even with my hopeless sense
of direction, without benefit of GPS coordinates or even Google Maps,
I will always   find you   there.

Clarifying the protection of birds legislation

Vanessa Lampert

Cats must be surrendered with immediate effect.
Cats that once belonged to a relative you adored are not exempt.
Cats called Mr Binks, Mr Fluffytoes or Mr (insert any word here)
are not exempt. Cats bearing a name with the suffix 'kin or kins'
eg Scrummykins, or Mummy's Fluffyboykin are not exempt.
Cats with names that bridge the prefix Mr and the suffix kin(s)
eg Mr Teddykins, are especially not exempt.
Cats with human names like Ian, Linda or Neil, all indoor cats
and cats that go out but come in to defecate are nor exempt.
Pedigree cats including Norwegian Forest, Birman, Australian Mist,
Balinese, Chartreux, Turkish Van, Tonkinese, Siberian Forest,
Scottish Fold, or any cat you paid for, or arranged payment in kind for,
are not exempt.
All kittens, cats who sleep in your bed with you, any cat
you have found with its head on your pillow and its body under the duvet,
all cats with bells on their collars that tinkle when they scamper,
cats that can lift a prawn from a champagne flute with their non-dominant
front paw, cats that miaow when a lion appears on TV,
all these cats are not exempt.
Cats that have climbed into a tumble drier, narrowly escaping
death, cats who prefer your food, cats that wait for you to turn the tap on
so that they might daintily drink, cats that drink from the toilet, cats
that suddenly rush across the room without reason, all cats with issues
that may or may not have been driven to a consultation
with a cat psychologist are not exempt.
Exempt cats must have demonstrated that they have no
desire for,
or active involvement in the killing of birds, and/or must not
have been recently learning how, and might thus have henceforth
been theoretically responsible for the imminent killing of birds.
Exempt cats must have shown beyond reasonable doubt that they have
no wish to gain or regain the speed and/or stealth necessary
to exterminate as many birds as can be pulled from the sky,
as evidenced by being found to be in possession of teeth designed for tearing,
paws full of oft-sharpened knives for cutting, and minds devoted
to carefully constructing plans for, the tremendous suffering of birds.
Killing all the birds. Making the birds pay. Doing it slowly

Every Black History Month

Wura Arisekola

Every Black History Month your people scream
Join us as we celebrate black excellence!
Join us as we highlight black voices!
Join us as we worship black girl magic!
Join us as we bask in black boy joy!

Every Black History Month my people plead
Join us as we bury the bodies of
George Floyd and Breonna Taylor and the foetus of Charleena Chavon Lyles and Charleena Chavon Lyles and David McAtee and Dreasjon Reed and Michael Brent Charles Ramos and Manuel Elijah Ellis and Atatiana Koquice Jefferson and Emantic Fitzgerald Bradford Jr. and Charles Roundtree Jr. and Chinedu Okobi and Botham Shem Jean and Antwon Rose Jr. and Saheed Vassell and Stephon Alonzo Clark and Aaron Bailey and Jordan Edwards and Chad Robertson and Deborah Danner and Alfred Olango and Terence Crutcher and Terrence LeDell Sterling and Korryn Gaines and Joseph Curtis Mann and Philando Castile and Alton Sterling and Bettie Jones and Quintonio LeGrier and Corey Lamar Jones and Jamar O'Neal Clark and Jeremy McDole and India Kager and Samuel Vincent DuBose and Sandra Bland and Brendon K. Glenn and Freddie Carlos Gray Jr. and Walter Lamar Scott and Eric Courtney Harris and Phillip Gregory White and Mya Shawatza Hall and Meagan Hockaday and Tony Terrell Robinson Jr. and Janisha Fonville and Natasha McKenna and Jerame C. Reid and Rumain Brisbon and Tamir Rice and Akai Kareem Gurley and Tanisha N. Anderson and Dante Parker and Ezell Ford and Michael Brown Jr. and John Crawford and Eric Garner and Dontre Hamilton and Victor White and Gabriella Monique Nevarez and Yvette Smith and McKenzie J. Cochran and Jordan Baker and Andy Lopez and Miriam Iris Carey and Barrington Williams and Jonathan Ferrell and Carlos Alcis and Larry Eugene Jackson Jr. and Kyam Livingston and Clinton R. Allen and Kimani Gray and Kayla Moore and Jamaal Moore and Johnnie Kamahi Warren and Shelly Marie Frey and Darnisha Diana Harris and Timothy Russell and Malissa Williams and Noel Palanco and Reynaldo Cuevas and Chavis Carter and Alesia Thomas and Shantel Davis and Sharmel T. Edwards and Tamon Robinson and Ervin Lee Jefferson and Kendrec McDade and Rekia Boyd and Shereese Francis and Jersey K. Green and Wendell James Allen and Nehemiah Lazar Dillard and Dante' Lamar Price and Raymond

Luther Allen Jr. and Manual Levi Loggins Jr. and Ramarley Graham and Kenneth Chamberlain Sr. and Alonzo Ashley and Derek Williams and Raheim Brown Jr. and Reginald Doucet

You never do.

If I had a lodger I could explain

Tamsin Hopkins

how there's never the right amount of coffee left,
how the peanut butter has been scraped away differently,
the surprise of evaporated shampoo. The windows
are suddenly speckled, unknown dust-balls appear
like fallen nebulae, drowsy with improbable time.

Sometimes the dog barks for no reason,
her ladylike yips echoing down the hall.
We wait together for steps to crunch on gravel,
the lift and flip of the letterbox, but no–
it's the roof-moss throwing itself onto the path again.

This *is* my house, I know it,
but somehow it has shifted, slid away from me,
it has got cocky, brassy, revealing scuffs
and scratches I am not familiar with,
a biro mark on the sofa I do not think was me.

It's Autumn again, the neighbours' children lope past,
newly lanky, crisp in their uniforms. Some even wave
and I wave back, trowel in hand. Halloo, how you've grown.
Who are you? I whisper to the privet, to the pink and white
heathers I am planting.

Jenny Wren

Ben Verinder

A bobbing bright-eyed ball of songbird
in the hedge beside my house flings its chirrs
and scolds, notes sharp and hard as the tail end
of a terracotta wren on which my mum
hung her wedding ring when washing up.
This was her nickname among school friends
spotted in the foliage of Christmas cards
and a phrase I heard my father use just once
as he knelt beside the humming car
lifted her easily into the house
her gown opened like curtains to display
the welts where drunken mummer cells
performed the metastatic dance
of a wren-hunt on St Stephen's day.

Lost Girls

Federica Peru

Where do the lost girls go?
The girls walking on clouds
Because the ground cuts their feet
And wants them kneeling on blades,
The girls with bold bald heads
Because fists used to bury themselves in their hair
And tug their scared, enraged gaze towards the sky,
The girls who went into the woods
And never walked out, because brambles and bears
Are less dangerous than men.

Where do the lost girls go?
The girls who make stories out of screams
And spells out of leftover chicken bones,
The girls that carry children on their back
And in their belly and know deeply
That loving someone does not make you free.

Where do the lost girls go?
The girls rolling around, pearls from a broken necklace,
With their high heels and their bare feet,
Running towards hidden horizons,
Holding each other up when the storm comes,
With their wild eyes and tongues they bite no longer,
With blood flowing freely down their legs?

Where do the lost girls go?
Is there a Neverland for them too?

Manarola – final night – no camera

Han Smith

The tame between inhale and cleft surface –
descending for that pale, far thing: mood,
a darkness to obscure these skins to nude
and back again, and over, and curvings
of a tighter water. This, too, a current;
this, too, a need, before time is out and
breath must end. The sunken city, mountain
range, gold-locked treasures of the mind-summoned
dive are mirage, dissolved, when what holds strong
this deep is how yet to be suspended,
pared. Until the up-fled surge – our sea-shine,
uneyed, immense, and a never tendered
touch, but softer still: a liquid meantime.
This, too, the current; this, too, the need-song.

The Promised Land

Maia Béar

When I first saw you and it took my feet out from under me,
red-black hair taking all the sun out of the Magdalene practice room,
when I saw your bird collar-bones beneath
white daisy-print breathing up and down
like the leaves of a book or the flickering
stream of matzo meal pouring through
my mother's paper fingers of
freckles and Kiehl's orange-balm softness,
when I saw that then I was made glad,
and the gladness poured out of me all in a rush
like when the sea took two deep gasps
and we passed through on our way home,
when I saw your hair it was like that,
it was like that but better.

A Short Film About Love

Joseph Kidney

I am a human being; of that which is human
I think nothing estranged from me.
-Chremes, *The Self-Tormentor*

Common to all forms of nursing
—a slowness, careful, a slow care—
is how he watches her remove
the carton from the paper bag
and the eggs from the carton.
On the nights she cries he thinks
about how a coat loses its shape
when you hang it on a hook
and other types of storage
that resemble collapse. Then
he strokes himself until he startles.
Covering the telescope with canvas
he wonders what kind of contact
eyes make—how a crime could
provide its own alibi. He'd stolen
the device from the high school,
taking a hammer to a window
which dropped like the salt she strews
on the meat unswaddled from paper.
This is meant to rearrange the blood.
There's a reason for pouring salt
in a wound. It tastes so much better.

2020 YOUNG WRITERS' POETRY AWARD
PRIZE WINNER

Young Writers' Poetry Award Judge's Report

Cameron Stuart

It is an honour to be asked to judge this year's young poets award, and despite myriad difficulties and testing circumstances, we had well over 250 entries in this category alone. These poets have shared their words from all around the UK and indeed, all around the world, and it's been inspiring that so many poets have turned their hand at producing these submissions, revising, reconstructing and submitting them too, in what has undoubtedly been one of the toughest times in living memory. With these new restrictions and an ever-evolving new articulation of "normal" life, it's been fascinating to see people interrogate that covid space, as well as break out of it. In terms of the former, it's been fascinating that so many of these poems are about wielding new lenses and weaving new magic into previously domestic, samey, and mundane spaces. These poems have found themselves formed through intense hyper locality, casting some intense poetic thought onto the spaces that many of us have come to view/inhabit/commune with on a daily basis.

Equally, people have used history and mythology and sci fi and surreality to abscond from the pandemic's restrictive hand, and it has been marvellous to witness the ability of poetic thought and practice to permeate those kinds of spaces and to offer new opportunities for exploration. I want to particularly commend the poets that have spoken towards social activism. Also the poets that have tried new forms, or indeed, as Angela Carter might put it, 'pour new wine into old skins' with some of their formwork. The entries speak to the quality of formal and informal poetic shapes, and I was lucky to have the difficulty of navigating many works that pushed against convention, as well as many poems that showcased great skill at traditional poetic forms.

If I could have a whole cohort of winners, I would. The poem that I have picked suffuses both the domestic space and the restrictions that the last year has brought, but at the same time exploded it with the ecstatic possibility of the personal and the eloquent possibility of the epic. The poem is an intense personal essay that also seems to utilise found materials, classic imagery, and confessional register. There are just so many memorable lines in this piece, moments that feel incredibly lush and lyric, sweet, small, human moments, and yet also moments that are stained with possible transgression, and with an oppression and oppression and violence. The poem rallies against, fights for, and bears witness, all in a movingly believable singular voice. I think the way that the poet has been able to definitely weave through those different tonal qualities in this poem really speaks to their ability on a craft level, but also to their intensely personal, enjoyable, believable voice. Congratulations to Alba Alonso Palombi for her winning poem *Mi Muerde Duende*.

Mi Duende Muerde

Alba Alonso Palombi

I am

and I am hunted by magpies and dogs that howl after the night hugs the first rays of sun almost a still birth of light; catching the breath before everything turns white

and I am strongest when I am vulnerable and I show what I have contained and marinated in the pot of my ribcage to the eyes and ears of those who can't bear blame

who loves the moon and called out the October-light and her spell

who sees everything green and red and who cannot bear any charity weight

who is ruled and watered by ink and conjures remnants in cities where she's never been and who somehow still has a lot of love to give

who stays up at night looking at shooting stars in August-terrace and wishes the same four things

who brought an ashtray to her lips desperate for the taste of his kisses that had left with the summer

who had to be hurt and hurt and hurt and hurt and hurt to realize that maybe what she saw was not worth it

who is enchanted and homes a duende with knifing wings and sharp teeth that finds her sweet spot and bites it till she bleeds because her *DUENDE MUERDE*

who cannot and will not go on without feeling and will glue the pieces back together because it is all about *kintsugi*

who knows wet dogs will bite you twice as hard and that you have to gift your distraught to those who will not let it stop

who says she has forgiven his house but really wants his bed to stay empty

who wears her grandma's coat and her grandpa's glasses and who loves to dance when everyone's watching who climbs on rooftops and gets her friends to scream with her and scares the magpies when they come in pairs

who writes in the dark and reads to herself and then lets him hear what her pillow drowned and felt his tear drops from the squeeze of his hand-hold

who draws constellations in his moles and traces a map and writes *AND DOGGEZ TO DETHE INDITE* on his arm because *MUERTO EL PERRO SE ACABÓ LA RABIA* but the hounds always know and when you run they chase you because they think it's a game and then they become *HORTELANO*'s because they neither eat nor let you

and who loses herself in those she wants to have and love and makes them a priority like a glittering prize of gold and morphs herself into the podium

who pierced and pierced her skin spending 20 to 25 euros per hole basking in the change in pain and who only took out the steel after she was not controlled by a him

who knows that the sea is pink because of the church burning in the hill, and that when you are haunted you just have to tell the ghosts to leave

I am.

2020 BEDFORD POETRY PRIZE WINNER

Bedford Poetry Prize Judge's Report

Steve Kendall

I was very happy to be asked to be a judge of the Bedford Poetry Prize, because I have a long association with Bedford and with its strong and diverse poetry scene. The poem, *October*, that I chose as the winner, jumped straight out at me. I particularly enjoyed the image of months as rivers and was impressed by the way the poet used the natural world to convey difficult, unwelcome feelings.

We are accustomed, I suppose, to poems about lost love and the passing of the seasons, but we don't necessarily expect to encounter a word like rot in poems on that kind of topic, but there it is, at the end of the first stanza, signalling the fate of the unwanted foliage, weak branches, and unpicked, dried berries of the next stanza.

In places the imagery is more conventional, but this reminded me of the way a folk song has familiar features, such as the way we come across the small birds that sing in the May morning, in that kind of song, and it was therefore appropriate in its context, and did not tip the poem over into sentimentality. The closing lines bring us back to the river and the passing months, and they do so in simple, direct, fresh language. I thought this was an engaging affecting poem, a highly promising piece of work.

October

Maya Abraham-Steele

I lie on my back
In October's river
And let the pull of the new moon
Wash over the rot in me

The trees shed unwanted foliage,
Unpicked, dried berries and
Branches too weak to see
The first frost

When I met him, the blossom was coming in
The gentle rays of the sun
Teased me with a promise
Of more to come

Fledglings – small and terrified –
Greeted me as I began
A journey of
Introspection

He stayed through the warm months
The beers by June's river months
The still light at eleven months
The this feels like heaven months

But he left before the harvest.

Biographies

Maya Abraham-Steele is a graduate from the University College London (UCL) gaining a BA (Hons) in English Language and Literature and BPP University with an MSc in Psychology. Maya grew up in Bedford, where she currently lives and works as an Assistant Psychologist. Writing is a long term passion of Maya's and she has written since childhood, first gaining recognition by the Tower Poetry Society at Oxford University aged 18.

Throughout her undergraduate studies her poetry was published by university journals and publications and she has written professionally, previously working as a Communications and Marketing Officer at UCL. Maya continues to be an avid writer of both poetry and prose and is currently working on both a poetry collection and a full length novel. She takes inspiration from her life experiences, exploring themes such as navigating the transition from girlhood to womanhood, self-hood and other, love, sexuality, home, childhood bereavement and loss, and the every day. Maya is fascinated by the human condition and hopes to make a career of creative writing, alongside her career in psychology.

Norma Allen has always enjoyed writing and now is lucky enough to be able to do so from her hill-top summer-house overlooking the Severn Valley in rural Mid-Wales. Since she and her husband moved back to Wales, following her retirement as a Special Needs teacher, she has gained an MA in Creative Writing from the University of Wales, Aberystwyth. She regularly contributes to the village magazine and writes stories and articles for Pencambria, the Mid-Wales magazine of History, Heritage and Literature, as well as entering the odd writing competition. She is very pleased to have been placed in this one.

Wura Arisekola lives in Ireland with her family. She has always had a great love for poetry, and her favourite poets are Seamus Heaney and Eavan Boland. Last year, she decided to start writing some poems of her own. Every Black History Month is one of the first poems that she has ever written.

Maia Ruth Béar is a poet and musician based in north London, where she has lived all her life. She studied English at Trinity College, Cambridge, and is now studying for a PhD in Medieval literature at Yale University. She started writing poetry in 2019 to prove that she could, and has since been published in Uncustom Definitive magazine and performed her poetry live at the George Tavern in Shadwell. Her poems have been performed and recorded by young composers both classical and experimental.

Maia's influences include Ada Limón, Gerard Manley Hopkins, Ted Hughes, and Geoffrey Hill, as well as scripture and liturgy; her work moves between genres and modes, drawing on confessional, devotional, and abstract patterns of writing and thought. She is often concerned with the relationship between place and memory. Outside of writing poetry, she enjoys playing rugby for her beloved Hampstead Ladies RFC; she is most proud of writing one of their team songs.

Chris Barkley is an award-winning writer, with prose published in TSS, Palm Sized Press and the Writers of the Future 35th anthology. He has been shortlisted for the Cambridge Short Story Prize and his poetry has featured in Agenda and Wet Grain. He has also won The Stage Award at Edinburgh Fringe. After graduating from Warwick University with a First, he is currently studying an MSt in Creative Writing at Oxford University. He also works for a charitable foundation, using creative writing as a tool for social outreach. His writing is concerned with the act of storytelling, our relationship with nature, and how we interact with time. His twitter is @TufferBarkley and his website is www.chrisbarkley.co.uk

Robert Carter is an Australian writer who has won international awards for his work and received outstanding reviews from around the world. His first novel, *The Sugar Factory*, published in US, UK, Australia etc. won the Angus & Robertson Fellowship and was shortlisted for the Miles Franklin Award and 2 Premier's Awards and translated into several languages. A collection of short stories, *The Pleasure Within* and a novel, *Prints in the Valley*, followed to international acclaim. Published as a YA novel, *The Collectors*, was shortlisted for the CBC Book of the Year and won the National Human Rights Award (Chdns. Lit.).

As film writer/director, Robert won Best Feature Film at the Hollywood Film Festival in 1998, adapting his own novel. He has been awarded residencies and Fellowships to La Cité internationale des arts in Paris, Yaddo, New York and to Los Angeles. He wrote and directed the feature film, *Thirst* to critical acclaim in 2012. He has taught in several universities and has published poetry and short stories in various national and international journals, including Oxford University Press, Critical Quarterly (UK), Meanjin, Southerly, Bridport prize, Montreal prize, Best Australian Poems series. www.thirstthefilm.com.

Anne Casey is originally from the west of Ireland and now lives in Sydney, Australia. She is an award-winning poet, writer and author of two critically acclaimed poetry collections – *where the lost things go* (Salmon Poetry 2017) and *out of emptied cups* (Salmon Poetry 2019), with two books forthcoming in 2021. Her second collection was selected for *Best Dressed* in 2020 by Sundress Academy for the Arts in the USA – the curators of the prestigious *Best of the Net* awards. This book was also selected for *Books of the Year 2019* by *The Lonely Crowd* magazine in the UK.

Anne has worked for 30 years as a journalist, magazine editor, media communications director and legal author. Her essays, articles and poetry are widely published internationally and rank in *The Irish Times* newspaper's Most-Read. She has won/shortlisted for poetry prizes in Ireland, Northern Ireland, the USA, the UK, Canada, Hong Kong and Australia – including the *ACU Prize for Poetry, Henry Lawson Poetry Competition, Women's National Book Association of USA Poetry Competition, Atlanta Review International Poetry Contest, 25th Annual Melbourne Poets Union International Poetry Competition, Hennessy New Irish Writing, Cúirt International Poetry Prize, Overton Poetry Prize, The Plough Prize, Bedford International Writing Competition, Tom Collins Prize (Fellowship of Australian Writers, Western Australia)* and *Fellowship of Australian Writers Queensland Literary Competition.*

Anne's poems feature internationally in newspapers, magazines, journals, anthologies, podcasts, music albums, stage shows and art exhibitions – including *The Irish Poetry Reading Archive* (James Joyce Library, University College Dublin), *The Irish Times, The Canberra Times, Australian Poetry Anthology, Beltway Poetry Quarterly, Atlanta Review, Tahoma Literary Review, Quiddity, Entropy, The Murmur House, Barzakh* (State University of New York), *Connecticut River Review, The Stony Thursday Book, Westerly Magazine* and *Cordite Poetry Review* among many others. She has been nominated for the 2021 *iWoman Global Award* in the field of Literature and for the *Pushcart Prize.*

A frequent headliner at literary events, conferences and universities, Anne has given reading tours in Australia, Ireland and the USA. She has featured at fixtures including the State Library of New South Wales; Ireland's largest and longest running traditional music summer school and festival, Scoil Samhraidh Willie Clancy; one of Europe's oldest and most respected literary festivals, Cúirt International Festival of Literature (Galway, Ireland); AWP, the largest bookfair and conference in North America; Poetry Ireland (Dublin, Ireland); the University of Missouri-St Louis; the University of Newcastle (Australia); Swinburne University (Melbourne); and the University of Canberra.

Anne holds an honours Law Degree from University College Dublin and qualifications in Media Communications from the Technological University Dublin, where she graduated First Place in her class. She is undertaking a PhD in Creative Writing at the University of Technology Sydney, supported by an Australian government scholarship.

Website: anne-casey.com Social media: @1annecasey

Paul Chiswick spent his childhood years in Manchester, Chepstow and Cheshire. After attending university in Yorkshire and qualifying as an engineer he began work back in Cheshire followed by landing jobs in parts of Asia and finally Hong Kong. After so much travelling he decided it was time to settle down and start a family back in Britain but, at the same time, he sought a career change and moved into IT sales.

Twenty-five years later, he retired from corporate life in order to pursue his love of writing. Four novels and many short stories later, it has proven to be a pleasurable way to pass those free hours when not pursuing the 1001 other activities that seem to fill a retiree's life.

He and his wife now live in a Warwickshire village, close by his only daughter. More information about his works and achievements can be found at www.paulchiswick.com

Anya Christiansen loves to write and is so glad that there is such a wonderful international community where she can pursue that passion with so much support. It helps her believe that her dream of one day becoming an author might not be entirely impossible after all.

At the moment though, she is just excited to write anything at all and hopes her near-constant writer's block disappears with age and experience. She also loves reading, singing and anthropology. She is eighteen and has just finished her last year of secondary school. Her next goal is surviving university and finishing a Law and Global Studies conjoint, while still keeping up with her stories. She is so thrilled about her creative writing future and is very excited for the world that awaits her.

Sarah Dawson grew up in Kent and, apart from a four-year stay in the US, has never left. She has a degree in English and, before having children, spent six years in book publishing – at Hodder & Stoughton and Darton Longman & Todd – where she worked first in editorial and then in publicity. Since then, she has worked as a freelance copy editor and proofreader, a play-worker at an after-school club, a volunteer at a soup kitchen and as a reading helper with the literacy charity, Beanstalk. She loves dogs, particularly greyhounds, which often feature in her stories.

In 2019 she won the Colm Tóibín International Short Story Award, and in 2018 was shortlisted for it. Mostly, though, Sarah writes novels. Her modern retelling of *Tess of the d'Urbervilles* (*The Boy Who Wouldn't Hurt a Fly*) was shortlisted for the Exeter Novel Prize (2016) and long listed for the Bluepencilagency First Novel Prize (2017). Her second YA novel – about a dog with a talent for finding murder victims (*The Violet Hour*) – was also shortlisted for the Exeter Novel Prize (2018) and longlisted for the Guppy Books YA Novel Competition and *Mslexia*'s Novel Competition (both 2020).

Her Unused Smile is Sarah's first foray into historical fiction and she loved the process of researching as well as writing it. She plans to do a lot more!

She is a member of an immensely supportive and talented writing group called ninevoices (do check out their blog: ninevoices.wordpress.com).

Amanda Hildebrandt has worked as a Script Reader, television Scriptwriter, and Media Analyst. Her film scripts and short fiction have won several awards, including the Grace Marion Wilson Emerging Writers' Prize and the UCLA Students' Prize. Amanda has just completed her biggest writing project to date: a 100,000-word doctoral thesis on flight attendant uniforms. In her downtime, she likes to eat tapas and play the violin.

Juliet Hill worked as a theatre musician in the UK for twenty years before moving to Madrid where she started to write. She has written a number of short stories including *Laughing Boy*, a prize-winner in the Writer's Forum magazine competition; *Property is The*ft, shortlisted in the Fiction Desk Newcomer Prize 2015 and a runner-up in the Storgy Magazine´s 2015 short story competition; *Parka Billy*, shortlisted in the Highlands and Islands Short Story competition 2015, commended in the Southport Writer's Circle Short Story Competition 2016 and published in the Momaya Press Short Story Review 2020; *The Psychiatrist and the Cleaner,* highly commended in the Segora Short Story competition 2016 and shortlisted in the Earlyworks Press 2018 Competition; *Truth or Dare*, also shortlisted in the Earlyworks Press Competition; *Untroubled Waters*, a prize-winner in the Southport Writer's Circle Short Story Competition 2020. She is currently working on a novel.

Sophie Holland loves writing and reading in equal measure, and has been writing short stories and plays for the last ten years. Her favourite recently read collection is Elizabeth McCracken's 'Thunderstruck'. She completed a thoroughly enjoyable MA in creative writing at Oxford Brookes in 2017. In 2019, she won first and third prize in '1000 words' and Writer's Bureau short story competitions, so this completes the trio. She has performed her short fiction in Bristol, Bath and Oxford, and her short plays have been performed at Neath Little Theatre and the Rondo Theatre, Bath. She has a story in 'Stories from the Greenhouse' published by Comma Press, and more on her website sophieholland.org. She is about to start work with an editor on the completed first draft of her first novel. Away from writing, she works in Bristol part time as a speech and language therapist specialising in voice disorders, and tries hard (though often fails) to keep up with her three teenagers.

Tamsin Hopkins won the Aesthetic Creative Writing Award for poetry in 2020. She is currently studying part-time for a Creative Writing MA at Royal Holloway. Her poems have been published or are forthcoming in *New Statemsan, The Interpreter's House, Finished Creatures*, Eyewear *Best British and Irish Poets 2019-21*and a variety of competition anthologies. Her pamphlet *Inside the Smile* and her short story collection *SHORE TO SHORE* are published by Cinnamon Press.

Joseph Kidney is a Canadian writer and PhD candidate in Renaissance drama at Stanford University. His poems have appeared in *Vallum, The Fiddlehead, The New Quarterly*, and *PRISM*. He placed second in *Grain*'s Short Grain Contest and won The Young Buck Poetry Prize from *CV2* for the best poem submitted by an author under 35. He is intermittently active on Twitter @josephkidney2.

Vanessa Lampert has an MA in Writing Poetry from Newcastle University and Poetry School London. In 2020 she came first in the Café Writers and Ver prizes and was second in the Fish and International Oxford Brookes prizes. She was also commended in the Troubadour, Folklore, Segora and Newcastle poetry prizes. She recently won the Edward Thomas foundation prize 2021. She is currently working on her first full collection

Vanessa is a poetry tutor for Learning with Leaders, teaching children in India and she co-edits the online and print magazine The Alchemy Spoon. Her first pamphlet 'On Long Loan', was published by Live Canon in October 2020.

She works as an acupuncturist in Wallingford Oxfordshire.

Fran Maciver was formerly a Hertfordshire resident and, since 2016, has lived in retirement by the river in Bedford. She has two children and two, lovely grandchildren. She has been writing stories for the last twenty years, writes everyday and 'couldn't live without doing so'. Her output, to date, has sadly gone unrecognised by publishers, or those amazing people called 'agents', but she 'plods on'.

She enjoys writing children's stories with an historical bias, for 7-9 and for 9 -12-year-olds, covering such themes as the 'Secret Spitfires' of the Second World War; in 'Mirror Daughter', a Celtic mirror that allows 'time-slip' to Roman Britain and 'The Golden Eye of Saint Enica', in which a troubled 12-year-old boy, befriended by a pensioner, finds a Saxon brooch. ('Mirror Daughter' - published as a Kindle Book).

Fran belongs to a great writing group that met once a month, (before Covid) in the Cecil Higgins Museum & Art Gallery and presently meets online – 'they keep me encouraged and focused'. She writes and enjoys poetry – Wendy Cope; Dylan Thomas; Charles Causley.

Fran reads 'avidly, chiefly historical novels and detective stories, with a 'hunger' that is never satisfied'. Her ambition is 'not to own a Ferrari, but to see her writing enjoyed by children and the public in general.'

Her Bedford Competition short story, 'Barates and My Father', came out of her working background in Ethnic Minority Achievement in Hertfordshire and her Archaeology degree: 'a great deal of my heart went into that story'.

Isabella Mead won the 2019 Wells Festival of Literature Poetry Competition, judged by Simon Armitage. A former secondary English teacher in East London, she worked as a teacher trainer for two years in a rural Rwandan village before working in the learning departments of literary museums including the Roald Dahl Museum and Story Centre. As Head of Learning at The Story Museum in Oxford, she leads a vibrant team of storytellers and creative writing tutors. She holds a Masters in History of Art from the University of York and is currently studying for a degree in French, Italian and Spanish through the Open University.

Isabella won second prize in the 2020 Segora International Poetry Competition. She has been Highly Commended twice in the Bridport Prize (2016 and 2019) and shortlisted four times. She has also been Highly Commended in the Café Writers Prize (2018), the Mslexia Pamphlet Competition (2017) and longlisted in the National Poetry Competition (2017) and shortlisted for an Eric Gregory Award (2009). Her work has been published in *Poetry News, Magma, Mslexia* and *Envoi,* and also appears in anthologies including *Beyond the Storm: Poems from the Covid19 Era* (Write Out Loud, 2019), *Black Lives Matter: Poems for a New World* (CivicLeicester, 2020), *The Golden Book: 50 Years of Arvon* (The Arvon Foundation, 2018), and *Bollocks to Brexit: An Anthology of Poems and Short Fiction* (CivicLeicester, 2018). Website: www.isabellamead.co.uk

David Shelley Jones is pleased to have two stories short-listed for The Bedford 2020 1 Short Story Competition. He started writing a few years ago when his children were grown up and his medical practice in Sydney well-established. He won the Medical Journal of Australia MJ Dark National Short Story Competition in 2014 and the Bath Short Story Competition in 2018. He was long-listed for the 2020 Bristol Short Story Prize. Before this, his publications were on gynaecological surgery and obstetrics, so he is enjoying the latitude of fiction.

While city-based, David likes to spend as much time as possible "off the grid" in his caravan in southern New South Wales. He's also spent time working in outback towns and in the United Kingdom. With recent successes, he plans on devoting an increasing amount of time to writing short stories and novels.

Shirlee Smith Matheson has amongst her published work, eight aviation adventures, seven novels for young people and thirteen nonfiction books for adult readers, as well as short stories and stage plays. Aviation titles include: *Lost: Unsolved Mysteries of Canadian Aviation; Amazing Flights and Flyers*, and *Maverick in the Sky: The Aerial Adventures of WWI Flying Ace Freddie McCall*. (A three-book series, *Flying the Frontiers,* is currently out of print). In 1999 she won *The 99's Canadian Award in Aviation,* and is a charter member of *Canadian Women in Aviation International* (Rocky Mountain High chapter). A new edition of *This Was Our Valley*, regarding hydro-electric dams on the Peace River, was published in 2019.

Shirlee has lived in all four Western Canadian provinces. For many years she resided in the Peace River country of northeastern British Columbia. She currently lives in Calgary, Alberta, where she was employed for a number of years at the Aero Space Museum (now The Hangar Flight Museum).

Janet Newman writes stories and poems. She has enjoyed success in a number of national and international competitions. Some of her work has been selected for anthologies and has also been published in newspapers and magazines. Janet lives in Leicestershire where she is a member of Glenfield U3A Writers. When not writing, she walks, spends time in her garden and, to help stay sane during lockdown, is learning to play the ukulele.

Alba Alonso Palombi is an English Literature and Creative Writing finalist at the University of Warwick. She is originally from Madrid, where she grew up. She has also lived in the USA for three years. Her mother tongue is Spanish, which has a deep impact on her writing not only because of its rich tradition, but also because it puts some distance between her and the English language,letting her manipulate it ruthlessly. She writes ardently and prolifically about love and loss. She is working on her first poetry pamphlet, which she hopes to share soon. In the meantime, follow her Instagram account where she posts readings of her poetry, @thealbapoems.

Federica Peru is a 25 year old Italian student of Languages and Literature. She writes poems in English in spite of the challenges presented by a second language because it seems to encapsulate and convey her emotions in a peculiar, characteristic way that adds another layer of meaning to her words. The past few years have been useful practise for this craft, and the inclusion in this anthology, her first significant achievement in the field.

Pauline Plummer is an Irish /Welsh mixture from Liverpool who has lived in North East since the '80s where she brought up her family. She has two collections of poetry published, most recently 'Bint ', Red Squirrel Press, and a verse novella 'From Here to Timbuktu' Smokestack Press.

A collection of short stories, Dancing With a Stranger, 2015, Red Squirrel Press. She is a founding editor of Mudfog Press and has earned her living teaching creative writing, She cooks for a charity and works with refugees.

Harriet Sanders is a young writer of poetry and short fiction. In 2020 she graduated from the University of Canterbury with a Master of Writing, and she now plans to spend as much time writing as she can spare from her beloved horses.

With a degree in Classical Studies and English Literature, Harriet enjoys reading and researching myths from different cultures, and elements of these myths can often be found woven into her storytelling.

She has been nominated for awards by the New Zealand Poetry Society, TripFiction, and the Sunday Star Times.

She lives in Christchurch, New Zealand, and despite her English and Irish heritage identifies strongly as 'kiwi' – in solidarity with both the bird and the fruit.

Han Smith is a writer, translator and community literacy teacher, based in London. Shortlisted/longlisted for the Mslexia & Galley Beggar Press Novella Award, the Bridport Prize, the Desperate Literature Prize, the Brick Lane Bookshop Prize and the UEA New Forms Award, Han has also been published and commissioned by Versopolis, Hotel, Cipher Press, Litro, The Interpreter's House and the European Poetry Festival. Han was selected for a London Writers Award in 2019/2020 and is currently working on two novels. Twitter: @Han_Smiff; Web: www.han--smith.com

Kirsten Udall was born in Nuneaton in September 1999. She spent her first eighteen years in and around Coventry before moving to Exeter for her undergraduate degree in 2018. She is now working towards her final year creative writing dissertation, writing about a small boy who decides to investigate the mysterious "Witchy-Woo" next door. Pandemic-permitting, she is on target to graduate from the University of Exeter in July 2021 and then hopes to weasel her way to Edinburgh permanently in the coming years.

When she is not writing, Kirsten is reading, supporting her beloved Sky Blues or playing with her barmy dog, Barney.

To follow Kirsten's professional endeavours, her quest to make a life in Edinburgh and to support her future writing, you can find her at @kirstenudall on all social media channels, as well as linking with her on her LinkedIn page.

Molly Underwood was the winner of the 2019 Manchester Poetry Prize. Her work appears in the 2020 Aesthetica Creative Writing Anthology, and has been shortlisted for prizes including the Charles Causley International Poetry Competition and the Wells Open Poetry Competition. She is currently completing a Creative Writing MA at Goldsmiths, London.

Ben Verinder lives in rural Hertfordshire. His work recently won second prize in the 2021 Wolverhampton Literature Festival Poetry Competition, was commended in the Winchester Poetry Prize 2020 and shortlisted for the Buzzwords Poetry Competition 2020. Ben's poems have been published in Wild Court, Brittle Star, South, Obsessed with Pipework, Lighthouse, Ink Sweat and Tears, among others. He runs a reputation research agency and is the biographer of the adventurer and writer Mary Burkett.

James Woolf has seen his stories published widely, including Spread the Word, Storgy Magazine, Riggwelter, Village Square Journal, Cabinet of Heed and the New York horror magazine Coffin Bell. His fourth short story for Ambit magazine will appear in the July 2021 issue.

He considers short stories to be his science laboratory, a place for experimentation with form. He often seeks new ways to shape a narrative, such as in *R v Sieger – additional documents disclosed by the Crown Prosecution Service*, in which key events emerge through a bundle of court documents. In *A Tale of Twelve Speeches*, the story is rendered entirely through a collection of audition speeches for actors, and the footnotes of a mediocre playwright. *Good Morning, Azar* is based upon the notes left by a barrister to his cleaner.

James has been shortlisted for many competitions, including twice in the Bridport Short Story Prize and the Exeter Short Story Prize. He was placed second in the Greenacre short story competition, and highly commended in the London Short Story Prize.

He also writes scripts for the theatre and his most recent play, *Empty in Angel*, a one-woman play about the gig economy, was a finalist in two categories in the 2020 Standing Ovation awards. The play will be appearing at different venues when theatres reopen. He has also written radio plays for Radio 4 and LBC.

He is currently completing a novel, *Indefensible,* about a criminal barrister who becomes too close to a client he represented in a murder trial.

James lives in London with his family. His website is www.woolf.biz.

The Bedford Competition 2021

Let your talent flow and compete with authors from around the world! We invite you to submit stories up to 3000 words and poems up to 40 lines long.

1st Prize £1000 2nd Prize £200 3rd Prize £100

Short Story Judge - Patrick McGuinness
Poetry Judge - Anne Berkeley
Cygnature Short Story Prize - 17-25 yrs. - Katherine Mezzacappa
Cygnature Poetry Prize - 17-25 yrs. - Cameron Stuart
Bedford Short Story Prize - Guy Russell
Bedford Poetry Prize - Simon Wrigley

The Bedford Competition is a not-for-profit organisation. All net proceeds will go to Schoolreaders, Bedford, a charity giving free one-to-one reading support to children, and The King's Arms Homeless Project.

Competition opens 1st May and closes 31st October 2021.

To enter visit our website:

www.bedfordwritingcompetition.co.uk

Lightning Source UK Ltd.
Milton Keynes UK
UKHW010226210821
389184UK00001B/6

9 781838 258627